PORTAL24

MEREDITH STROUD

HOT
KEY
BOOKS

First published in Great Britain in 2013 by Hot Key Books
Northburgh House, 10 Northburgh Street, London EC1V 0AT

A CIP catalogue record for this book is available from the British Library.

ISBN: 978-1-4714-0210-4

1

Typeset by Palimpsest Book Production Limited, Falkirk, Stirlingshire
This book is typeset in 11pt New Caledonia

Printed and bound by Clays Ltd, St Ives Plc

FSC

Hot Key Books supports the Forest Stewardship Council (FSC),
the leading international forest certification organisation, and is committed
to printing only on Greenpeace-approved FSC-certified paper.

www.hotkeybooks.com

Hot Key Books is part of the Bonnier Publishing Group
www.bonnierpublishing.com

For Juniper, who loves me in
spite of my flaws,
and Vivian, who just thinks
they're funny.

Chapter One

Tourists always underestimated just how oppressive a Memphis summer could be. Locals crouched in the shade, watching as red-faced visitors in khaki shorts and expensive sandals realized for the first time why Southerners were 'lazy' and why the blues had grown out of the Mississippi's muddy banks. But to Darius Simms, the summer months weren't blue at all. No school meant no truant officers hassling him for cutting, and the influx of tourists meant easy money.

He stood behind a foldout card table at the corner of Second Street and Mulberry, running a single playing card across his knuckles like a leaf on a breeze. Darius had learned long ago that marks feared the well-dressed and friendly people almost as much as they did the shabby and angry. He rode the middle as hard as he could, choosing pragmatically rolled-up slacks and loafers with a white tank top and an untucked dress shirt. That was the game, really, making yourself look like you weren't trying too hard, and Darius was very good at it. He had been taught by the best, after all.

People had been walking by his table for nearly an hour now, casting curious glances but little else. Just as he was getting ready to pack up and let Zoe buy dinner after all, Darius found the answer to his prayers, in the form of the biggest poser he had ever seen. The man was a little over five and a half feet tall, and his sparse hair was shaped into immaculate spikes with frosted tips. He had a narrow line of beard running from ear to chin to ear, in what Darius assumed was an attempt to suggest the shape of a jawline, and he wore a shirt with Tony Montana from *Scarface* printed on it. As the man walked near the table, Darius snapped his card back into the deck.

'Yo,' he said.

The poser stopped, looked around, saw Darius, and then raised an eyebrow.

'Yeah, you, man. Where you headed?'

'Beale Street,' the man said after a moment of hesitation.

Darius leaned back against the wall and started cutting his deck. He shook his head and adopted a knowing, patronizing smile. 'Beale Street, man. And here I thought you looked cool.'

'What's wrong with Beale Street?' He stepped closer to the table.

'Nothing's wrong with it, if you wanna be a tourist. You just didn't have the look, is all.'

The man's face brightened at the idea that he could pass for a local. He was hooked, Darius could tell, but the trick was not to reel him in too fast.

'Listen, man,' Darius said. 'B Street don't have nothing for folks like us. You wanna have some real fun, you stick with me, yeah?'

'What did you have in mind?' the man said. He leaned against the table. 'Name's Owen, by the way. Friends call me O.G.'

Darius smiled, flipped his cards into his left hand, and held out his right. 'Cool. I'm Quincy. You ever run a hustle, Owen?'

The poser looked up and down the street, probably watching out for cops. 'Sort of. I mean, I listen to a lot of rap, and I'm a salesman, so—'

'Look, this ain't a job interview,' Darius said. 'You can just tell me no. Everybody has to start someplace, you feel me?'

'Yeah! Okay, well then, no, I've never been involved in one.'

'All right then. I'll tell you straight up, Owen, I usually don't trust somebody right out the gate like this, but all my regular boys bailed on me, and I got a need for some money, like, five minutes ago. So I need your help. You in?'

Owen looked up and down the street again. 'What do you need me to do?'

Darius stood up straight. 'You ever hear of three-card monte?'

'Yeah, I've seen it done once or twice.' Owen narrowed his eyes. 'You need a shill.'

'Awwwww, man, *shill's* such a dirty word. I need a confidant. A man-at-arms. A wingman. You're cool, right? I thought you was down.'

Owen held up his hands. 'No, man, no, it's cool. Just tell me what you need.'

'All right, good,' Darius said. He slid one hand into his pocket and hit SEND while he spoke, sending a pretyped message to Oscar, who was currently sitting in an air-conditioned coffee shop two blocks away. 'So here's how it goes: You play the game while folks walk by. You'll win a couple and lose a couple, but it'll look like the game ain't rigged either way. When I drum my fingers, that means you pick the left card. When I scratch my nose, you pick the middle card. You follow?'

Owen nodded.

'Good. So when a mark comes by and plays a couple games, you pull 'em aside and tell them you figured out what my tells are and let him think he can win. I'll give him the first couple of games, and then when he gets confident, I'll take him for all he's worth, and in the meantime you've left to take a walk around the block. And when you get back we start the whole thing over, got me?'

Owen nodded but looked a little dubious. All the same, Darius knew he wouldn't back out at this point.

'How much money you got? I don't wanna sketch you out or nothin', but we'll need to be trading real money back and forth or it won't seem convincing.'

'Oh, um,' Owen said, and there was that doubt again, but he pulled his wallet out anyway. Darius got a glimpse of a half-dozen shiny credit cards and a fat wad of twenty-dollar bills, and all his guilt melted away. Darius wasn't a communist or anything, but he'd met a lot of people in his life and as far as he'd ever seen, the amount of money people had was inversely related to how much they'd had to work to get it. Owen took a handful of the twenties from his billfold, placed them in his pocket, and looked at Darius expectantly.

'All right,' Darius said. His spine tingled with anticipation. He'd been wanting to try a three-card monte—with his own personal twist, of course. His father had always told him that the perfect crime is one that *isn't*, and like most of the man's advice, Darius hated how true it was.

'Let's get started.' Darius slapped three cards down on the table and started moving them around. 'The lady's elusive, my friend. The lady knows how to dance. She wants you something fierce, though, that she does. So follow the lady if you're man enough . . .'

He went on like that for about a minute each time, making a show of sliding the three cards around on the table. He finished his first rearrangement and slapped his hand down.

'The lady's in distress, my friend! Can you find the red lady?'

As Darius said this he rubbed his nose. Owen nodded and pulled out a twenty-dollar bill. Darius took it and stepped back as Owen lifted the middle card, revealing the red queen. Darius handed over Owen's twenty and another twenty he'd brought along as 'venture capital.' Then he started the game again.

This time, things went a little differently. Darius scratched his ear, Owen handed him a twenty and picked up the left card, and the queen was missing. Darius kept the twenty. Owen 'lost' the next game as well, thinking all the while that he was playing his part in a larger con—which was technically true. This went on for the next ten minutes, with Owen winning one round for every two he lost. He should have been breaking even, and he probably thought he was, but that was because he hadn't noticed that, after that first time, Darius had stopped giving him twenties back. By the time Oscar finally came around the corner, Owen had become the unwitting owner of a pocketful of one-dollar bills.

'What're y'all playin'?' Oscar said. He walked with a pronounced swagger, his hands jammed in his pockets. He was a tall, lanky kid about Darius's age. His head was shaved, and he wore a pair of aviators.

'Just a friendly game of chance.' Owen winked at Darius.

'Friendly, my ass!' Darius said. 'You're cleaning me out, man!'

'Whoa!' Owen said, holding up his hands. 'No hard feelings, okay? Luck's luck, after all. Tell you what though, I'm gonna make room for somebody else. It's like the gambler says: You gotta know when to hold 'em, know when to fold 'em, and, most importantly, know when to walk away.' He stood up, shook Darius's hand, and started to leave, but as he walked past Oscar he leaned in and whispered something. Oscar's eyes widened, and he nodded.

'Good t'know,' Oscar said. 'You have a good day now, man.'

Darius exchanged a look with Oscar and, as soon as Owen was out of sight, began packing everything up.

'How much?' Oscar said. He leaned against the wall and stretched lazily.

'Two hundred, I think. Haven't counted it yet. Should be about fifty for you, one-fifty for me.'

'Aw, how's that fair?'

'I did all the work,' Darius said. 'And besides, Zoe's leaving for New York tomorrow. You want me to take my girl out for a goodbye date with an empty wallet?'

Darius folded the table under his arm and stood—only to feel an intense wave of dizziness wash over him. It felt almost like déjà vu, but stronger than he'd ever known it before in his life. He looked around, trying to regain his bearings, and as he did he caught sight of a black Cadillac parked on the street corner.

A woman in a suit sat in the passenger seat, her eyes hidden behind a pair of dark sunglasses. At first it looked like she was asleep, but suddenly, those dark glasses turned toward Darius. Had that car been there the whole time?

Owen was probably five minutes from getting back, but Darius was still overcome by a sudden urge to sprint away. Instead, he forced himself to walk nonchalantly across the street.

'You okay?' Oscar asked, running to catch up, a note of concern in his voice.

Darius wasn't used to seeing his friend express emotions— beyond hunger or tiredness—and it only added to his agitation. An engine turned over behind him. He swiveled to look and watched, wide-eyed, as the black Cadillac drove slowly past.

The woman with the glasses waved without smiling.

Chapter Two

Darius was sitting on a bench in Confederate Park, reading a magazine he'd 'borrowed' from a nearby convenience store, when Zoe pulled up in her white Ford Mustang. She honked once and waved, grinning. Darius made a show of taking his time walking over and leaned in to rest his elbows on the window frame. 'Hey there, good lookin'. You headed my way?'

'Get in the car, doofus,' she said with a laugh. She was dressed practically for the heat in a floaty sundress and white sandals. Her platinum hair was tied back in a ponytail, but a few loose pieces framed the sides of her face. Her wicked green eyes were concealed by a pair of gigantic oval sunglasses Darius had gotten her as a joke in May, which she now refused to get rid of.

Darius hopped in the passenger seat and started to say, 'You ready to go out with a bang?' but he only got to 'ready' before noticing the same black Cadillac passing them.

'Ready for what?' Zoe said as the car turned a nearby corner.

'Nothing,' he said, shaking his head. 'Sorry, I just thought I saw somebody I knew.'

'Huh.' She twisted her lips cutely and looked at him over the top of her sunglasses. She drove the car lazily, barely paying attention, just her wrist rested against the wheel, and still never so much as swerved. 'Darius Simms, are you hiding another woman from me? Who do I need to kill before I can get a good night's sleep in New York?'

'Listen, honey,' Darius replied. 'I'm faithful as stone. True as an elephant. Solid as fact. Pretty much the most trustworthy guy south of the Mason-Dixon.'

She snickered and he shrugged, smiling.

'I mean, if you're still jealous, feel free to eliminate all the girls who want me. Don't know how Memphis'll get by without half its population, though.'

She laughed. 'I think the heat got to you.'

'Nah,' Darius said. 'Just hungry. What do you say we get the night started? I was thinkin' we'd hit Fat Cassidy's. It ain't nice like you deserve, but—'

'—but it's where you took me on our first date,' she said. 'I had indigestion for a week afterward. Worth it, though. You're lucky I'm such a romantic.'

'Don't I know it,' he said, and the reminder of that first evening sent a warm, tingling sensation down his back. He didn't know what he would do without her when she left for New York.

They found a leather booth by a window, red and cracked with age, and ordered some water. Zoe excused herself to the bathroom.

Just then, Darius noticed the same black Cadillac pull up on the street outside. He froze as the woman in the suit got out and entered the restaurant. She headed straight for his booth.

Without a word, she sat down across from Darius.

He couldn't help noticing that under her crisp dress shirt, she was carrying a gun. She took off her sunglasses, revealing dark circles under her eyes. Her blond bob looked dry and in need of a cut.

Darius opened his mouth to speak, but she held up a hand, pulled a pill bottle from a pocket inside her blazer, and shook three small white capsules into her palm. She swallowed them without water. Her mouth twitched once as they slid down her throat, and then her face shifted into an expression of bored neutrality.

'You've been following me.'

'Don't let it go to your head,' the woman said. The waiter dropped off the water and, thankfully, left without so much as raising an eyebrow. The woman gestured toward Zoe's water as if to say, *May I?* Darius nodded, and she took a long sip. A faint quaking in her shoulders betrayed just how thirsty she'd been.

'I haven't done anything illegal,' he lied.

She put the glass down after swallowing half its contents and returned her attention to Darius. 'I'm not here to arrest you.'

'So what do you want?' Darius said. 'Not to be rude or anything, but this is kind of my last night with my girlfriend for a long while.'

'Actually, you're never going to see her again after today. You're both going to die in a few hours.'

The sounds of the diner faded until all Darius could hear was his own pulse. He thought he had played it safe. He thought he had managed to avoid stepping on the toes of any of the hard criminals in his part of town—the gang-bangers and the dealers and the crooked cops.

He took a second to stop his hands from shaking. 'Do you make a regular habit of threatening teenagers?'

She gave a short, mirthless laugh. 'Yes, actually. This is not, however, a threat.'

'"It's not a threat, it's a promise," right? Have the decency to be original, at least.'

'Not a promise, either,' she said. She reached into another jacket pocket, pulled out a folded slip of paper, and slid it across the table. 'More like a warning. Promises and threats only apply when there's any question about an outcome.'

Darius picked up the paper and unfolded it carefully. It was a photograph of a bridge—it looked like the Hernando de Soto—with a white Ford Mustang disappearing over the side, flying toward the Mississippi River. In the image the vehicle had just flipped sideways over the guardrail. The front end was tipped sickeningly downward. It was a shocking enough image on its own, but what truly made Darius's blood run cold were the people inside the vehicle. The guy had dark skin and an Afro, and his dress shirt was spotted with red. The girl had blond hair—hair he recognized like it was his own. Both wore expressions of stark terror.

'You think this is funny?' he snapped, angrily folding the photo back up and tossing it onto the table. His voice cracked despite his efforts to control it, though he couldn't say whether it was from anger or fear.

'I've been told that my sense of humor is inadequate.'

'What's your angle? I never drove off that bridge. This picture is a fake. Proves nothing.'

The woman leaned forward and narrowed her eyes. 'What it proves is that I was there when it happens in about . . .'

She checked her watch. 'One hour, forty-three minutes, and seventeen seconds.'

'Ah,' Darius said, nodding slowly. So that was it. He wasn't dealing with a federal agent or a hired goon or even an angry former mark he'd forgotten about—she was just insane. And good at Photoshop. 'Well, that makes sense then. So you're from the future?'

'Yes.'

'And you came back to warn me.'

'Yes.'

'About a car accident I'm going to have this evening.'

'A fatal one.'

'Of course. And why me? Did I win the cosmic sweepstakes? Am I your father and you're trying to make sure I live long enough to marry your mom?'

'Well,' she said. She took another pill out of her pocket and swallowed it before continuing. 'Since you won't believe what I say anyway, I might as well tell you the truth: My name is Agent Grosz. I work for a top-secret government organization called Oberon that has access to an experimental method of time travel. The branch I work for is responsible for sending field agents back short distances through time to stop suitably catastrophic events before they have a chance to occur. One of our agents was . . . recently lost, and my job today is to recruit a new one.'

'Leaving aside the obvious question of why you would

want some no-name high school dropout for your super-secret organization, there's a pretty obvious hole in your story.'

'What's that?'

'Disasters happen all the time!' Darius threw his hands in the air. 'Not counting all the wars and famines and earthquakes and whatever else, if you're only looking at isolated attacks on innocent people, it seems like folks are getting killed every day.'

'I told you, Oberon only deals with suitably catastrophic events, and even then every precaution is taken to keep our actions secret. These aren't simple forces we work with—this is the space-time continuum, and there are still a lot of unknowns. It'd be nice if we could save everybody, but twenty lives isn't worth the possibility of rewriting history so the Nazis won.'

'Well, what about New York then? I don't know if you've seen the skyline lately, but something big is missing. You telling me that wasn't worth y'all's time?'

She pursed her lips and looked away. '9/11 is the reason Oberon was formed. The technology existed, but everyone was afraid to use it. A lot of lives could have been saved.'

'I'm moved. But you know I still don't believe you.'

'Of course you don't. You're a smart kid, and nobody's better at ignoring the truth.'

'My dad told me something similar once.'

'Wise man,' the woman said. She stood up and straightened her jacket.

'Not really,' Darius said. 'You two might get along, actually. If you weren't insane I'd say you might make a good hustler.'

The woman put her sunglasses back on and smiled. 'I work black-budget intelligence for the United States government,' she said. 'I've been hustling since I was fifteen.' She took a step toward the door, then turned back. 'So that's a no on the job offer?'

'I might consider it if the job actually existed, but since it doesn't . . .' Darius shrugged.

'By the way, in seven minutes a bird will ram into a pedestrian's head across the street from the window you're facing. Anyway, your girlfriend will be back in a few seconds, and I'd hate to ruin your last meal together. Be seeing you, Darius.'

She strode to the door, stepped outside, and disappeared into the crowd. He'd just started wondering what to tell Zoe when she appeared next to the booth.

'Who was that?' she said as she sat down across from him. 'Another name to go on my kill list?'

'Oh, no. Just a tourist.'

'Oh,' she said, her eyes narrowing. 'I see. What did she want?'

'Nothing. Directions. Wanted to know how to get to the bridge.'

'Mm,' she said. It was obvious that she thought he was lying.

'I'm sorry,' Darius said. 'I'm just kind of on edge, you know?'

'Yeah,' she said. Her face softened. 'I'm gonna miss you.'

'Me too,' Darius said, his stomach knotting up all at once. He felt an overwhelming sense of loneliness at the idea of being separated from Zoe. But the feeling was replaced by an awful, sinking dread when a few minutes later, a man across the street grabbed at his bloody nose and a cloud of feathers tumbled away through the air.

Chapter Three

'I wish you'd talk to me,' Zoe said.

'Hmm?' Darius kept his eyes on the road.

'Nothing.'

'I'm sorry, babe. I just got a lot on my mind.'

'And I don't?' she said. 'At least you get to stay here, with Oscar, with all your friends and familiar places. I'm going by myself to a huge city where no one even knows my name, and it's terrifying, and then on my last night with you, you're being all distant!'

He gave her a quick glance and the most penitent smile he could muster. From the look of disappointment she gave him, he guessed it probably hadn't been sincere enough. He pulled up to Mosby and Alabama with the left blinker on, only to find a traffic cop signaling for him to go right instead. He craned his neck to try to get a view of the obstruction, but he couldn't see anything. The same thing happened with every side street he came across; there was a roadblock on High Street, a car accident as he passed North Lauderdale. A ball of ice formed in Darius's stomach as each turn brought them closer to the river. And was he being really paranoid, or was a white van actually following them?

'I don't have to go to school,' Zoe said.

'That's insane,' Darius said. He was stunned enough to momentarily forget the crushing sense of danger. 'You've been talking about Juilliard as long as I've known you. You're the best musician I know.'

She smiled ruefully. 'When's the last time you listened to anything but blues and movie soundtracks?'

Another traffic cop appeared, directing him to turn again toward the fateful bridge. 'I know talent, and you've got it.'

'What about you?' she said. 'You could come with me and study film. You've got enough work online that you could probably get accepted anywhere.'

'You know I don't have the money,' Darius said. 'And I'm not taking any loans. I know a scam when I see one, and you'll pardon me if I'm not interested in being at the Man's beck and call for the next fifteen years.'

'Still,' she said, 'there are schools here, and it's not like my family would miss the money if they can't get my tuition back. Not to mention my apartment on Thirty-Eighth Street isn't exactly high-rent.'

'Would you really think about staying?' His hands tightened on the steering wheel. He wanted to tell her it sounded perfect. It *did* sound perfect. Still, he shook his head. 'No. I couldn't take that from you.'

Her voice, when she finally spoke, was small and quiet. 'It won't be forever. I'll wait for you.'

'You say that now,' Darius said, 'but we've never been apart this long.'

'You don't trust me?'

'I trust you. I really do. It's the future I don't trust.' He swallowed hard as another detour pointed him back to the one place in the city he didn't want to go. 'Like, what if it ends up being longer than we think?' Darius's forehead felt suddenly slick with sweat. 'Don't ask me why. Just . . . promise me you'll wait for me, even if we're separated a lot longer than a few months.'

She cocked her head curiously but put her left hand over his right and squeezed. 'I promise.'

'Okay,' Darius said. 'I love you.'

'I love you too, idiot,' she said. She shoved him playfully

and in the moment's distraction, he found himself entering the on-ramp for the interstate. It led directly toward the bridge.

Darius pulled to a complete stop at the top of the ramp, ignoring the angry honks from behind. Gazing into the rearview mirror, he noticed the white van again. Something told him he didn't want to see what was in that van, and that the best thing to do would be to get out of the car and try to run. He hated to admit it—in fact, he had been taught to believe that such situations didn't even *exist*—but for the first time in his life, Darius truly felt like there was no way out.

He put his foot on the gas and drifted forward. His heart sank as he rolled onto the overpass and saw, two cars behind him and a lane to the left, the black Cadillac, with Agent Grosz at the wheel.

As they reached the bridge, the Cadillac pulled up beside them and the van sped up behind, boxing them in. Darius flexed his hands on the wheel, his fingers going numb from the tightness of his grip. He bit his lip and looked out, past Zoe, into the void of the river beyond. Could they survive a fall like that? Would they be able to get out of the car before drowning? He drifted to the right, the sound of his breathing filling his ears. Would it improve their chances if he drove off now, carefully, instead of getting violently rammed off? The van stayed close behind him, certainly about to ram the Mustang's rear bumper. Darius sped up in response, drifting further to the right. Zoe was asking something, her voice loud and panicked, but he couldn't pay attention. Everything was slowing to a crawl and speeding out of control, all at once.

The shock of his tires grinding against the curb startled Darius back into focus. He looked one last time out at the river, and the faces in the picture—one of them his own—came back to him. Darius put his foot on the brake. Zoe was frantic now, pulling at his sleeve, but he couldn't look at her. He just swallowed and stared straight ahead.

The car came to a stop and he got out, the sound of his own heartbeat overpowering the honking of the traffic. Zoe got out of the car, calling after him.

He flagged down Agent Grosz. She stopped for him and opened the passenger door, her face expressionless. Darius turned and locked eyes with Zoe.

'Wait for me!' Darius yelled. 'You said you'd wait. You promised!'

'I don't understand!'

'I know,' he said as he got into the car, though she probably couldn't hear him. 'I'm sorry.'

He shut the door, and Agent Grosz put her foot on the gas. Darius watched Zoe in the side mirror. She stood in the middle of the road, the streetlights washing out all her color. Her hands rested at her sides, and her mouth was pulled into a straight line. Darius had a sudden, horrifying feeling that this was the last time he would ever see her. He was pulled out of the thought by Agent Grosz.

'Well?' she said. The look on her face was stern and neutral, but Darius thought he detected the faintest hint of sympathy in her voice.

'I'm in,' Darius said, as he watched Zoe disappear behind him.

Chapter Four

'Do you need any underwear?' Constance asked. She stopped and nodded at a store across the way.

Bianca Albert caught her reflection in the store's window and focused on it, doing her best to ignore the seminude lingerie models on display. She was short and lean, with well-muscled limbs developed from half a lifetime of gymnastics and martial arts training. Her face was pretty, she supposed, with its high cheekbones and full lips. But she always scowled when she saw her own reflection, drawing her eyebrows together and pursing her lips.

'I . . . don't need any, no,' she said. 'It's not like I have anyone to show off for.' She stopped at a kiosk that sold cheap cosmetics and picked up a hand mirror. She used it to discreetly observe the crowd behind them. The music coming through the speakers was bland and inoffensive, and the air conditioning was just a little too cold, causing the hairs on her arms and the back of her neck to stand on end.

'You sure?' Constance said. 'I heard they're bringing in a new recruit in the next couple of days. Might be cute. Never hurts to be prepared.'

Bianca shot Constance a look and walked quickly away from the kiosk. Constance, with her long legs, kept up easily.

'I'm sorry. I shouldn't have said anything. You know I don't think . . . I mean, he can't be replaced. That's not what it's about.'

Bianca closed her eyes and slowed down. She rubbed her forehead. 'Yeah,' she said. 'It just still hurts, you know?'

'I do,' she said. 'But I mean, life goes on.'

'Not for us.' Bianca hated being so relentlessly bleak, but her life was one long series of betrayals and disappointments. Her parents gave her to Oberon to avoid having to care for her. Her handlers and trainers, mostly ex-field agents them-selves, were emotionally distant if not actually cruel. She figured they had learned the same hard lesson she was now coping with. Isaac was gone, and one day she would be too.

Constance suddenly grabbed Bianca's wrist and pulled

her toward a nearby store. Bianca's muscles tensed, and her breathing quickened as she looked around. What had Constance seen that she'd missed?

'I don't know about *you*, but I'm desperate for some new heels,' Constance said. They came to a stop at the entrance of a brightly lit shoe store. Bianca willed her pulse to slow down as Constance strode down the nearest aisle, leaning close to examine a pair of red pumps.

Bianca stuck her hands in her pockets and followed a few steps behind, wondering what it was like to be a normal teenager. She'd spent more than half her life at the Nest, whereas Constance had joined their team much more recently. While Constance was having sleepovers, Bianca had been knee-deep in tactical manuals and combat-training regimens.

'Don't you think Malik is cute?' Constance said after a moment.

'I'm not really, you know—' she began, but a movement at the end of the aisle drew her attention.

One of the store clerks stood between them and the exit. His feet were planted wide, his eyes focused on Bianca and Constance. He reached to pull something out of a shoe box in his left hand.

Bianca narrowed her eyes, taking in his large build and close-cropped hair.

'*Down!*' she said. She grabbed a heavy work boot and

hurled it at the man. It bounced off his temple and he reeled, but not before firing two shots from the gun concealed in the shoe box. Bianca leaped down, ducking under the first shot, but the second hit Constance. The girl yelped and fell to the floor.

Bianca hurtled toward the assailant before he had time to recover from the boot. She jumped into the air, kicked off a nearby shelf, threw herself into a spin, and crashed her shin into his temple. He released a soft, confused 'Oof,' and joined Constance on the floor.

As she took stock of her surroundings, Bianca noticed the figures gathering outside the store: half a dozen men in helmets and body armor, carrying what looked like automatic rifles. One of them pointed at her the moment she saw them, and the others raised their weapons. Bianca vaulted backward. A hail of projectiles toppled the shelf where she had been standing moments before. She landed on her hands amid a shower of falling shoes, pushed off again, and hit the ground running toward the back of the store.

The bullets tore a line of destruction down the aisle as she ran. She took cover behind a shelf, pressing her back against it and listening intently. The bullets stopped, only to be replaced by the thunder of four pairs of clomping boots. Bianca calculated the length of the store, counted down, tensed her muscles, and waited.

Now.

She spun back into the aisle just in time to meet one of the assailants at arm's length. She wrenched his weapon to the side with her left hand and jabbed at his throat with her right, her fingers held straight and flat like a knife. He stumbled to the side, gagging.

There were four more men behind him—her count had been off. They stopped and raised their guns. Bianca spun forward and took cover behind the man. His allies all fired simultaneously, and his body shook violently before going still. His weight drooped onto Bianca's back, but she tolerated it for the few seconds it took her to check her new weapon and shoulder it.

Then, as easy as breathing, she stepped out, took aim, and planted two shots in two of the remaining men in as many seconds—one over the heart, one in the faceplate.

Both men tumbled backward. Bianca took aim for the third, but he already had a bead on her. He fired once and she was almost blinded by a blossom of red pain in her right shoulder. She fell against the racks and fired back, knocking the man into the wall, but then two more appeared in the aisle, weapons raised.

Bianca fired again, but her disabled arm couldn't handle the recoil and the pain threw off her balance, sending the shots wide. The men's shots were much more accurate; one hit her in the leg, and another hit her in the center of the chest. She fell backward, pulling boxes of pumps and sandals down on top of herself.

Her breath came in shallow, rasping gasps. The fluorescent lights on the ceiling faded in and out of focus.

Bianca was nursing the mother of all headaches as she neared one of the Nest's many conference rooms. She heard muffled voices behind the plain wooden door and braced herself before entering. The room was dark, a projector casting a flickering blue-and-white glow on the faces of everyone present. As Bianca entered, they all turned to look at her.

Director Spurling, a broad-shouldered man with a heavily lined, grizzled face, sat at the head of the table. Agent Grosz sat to his right, her demeanor projecting brisk, professional disinterest. Major Sturzer, the draconian tactical-control officer, sat to his left. His black uniform was immaculately pressed, his eyebrows drawn together to form a solid line.

Her three teammates were seated closer to the door. Constance had, as usual, recovered from the stun rounds incredibly quickly. She smiled and waved as though they had run into each other at a pep rally. Across from her sat Leon and Malik. Leon looked fine, except his glasses were missing. They had probably been broken during his tactical exercise. Malik had his forearms crossed on the table to act as a makeshift chinrest. The only acknowledgment he gave her was one raised eyebrow. She nodded in return as she sat down next to Constance. The stun hangover was usually as bad for him as it was for her, probably since they both tended to take multiple hits before going down.

Major Sturzer cleared his throat and raised his remote, directing their attention to his slides. 'As you can see,' he said, 'combat efficacy has remained essentially on a plateau. However, there is still the issue of Bianca's decline.'

Bianca was vaguely aware that her fingernails were digging lines across the wood of the table.

Sturzer tugged at his collar. 'Don't get me wrong,' he said. 'Your performance still vastly outstrips everyone in the exercise with the occasional exception of Malik, but we expect improvement.'

Bianca was about to fling her chair back and growl curses at Sturzer, but Director Spurling intervened before she had the chance.

'Now, now,' he said in his gravelly voice, 'it's all well and good to talk that way from where you're sitting, but maybe you don't remember what it's like to be young.'

'And you do?' Agent Grosz said.

Spurling either didn't hear or decided to ignore the comment. 'These fine young men and women seated with us are some of the most exceptional individuals on Earth, and I think sometimes you all forget how young they are. Why, it can't have been longer than what? A month, month and a half since Isaac was lost, and everyone knows how close Miss Albert was with—'

Bianca sat up straight in her chair. 'All due respect, sir, but I don't appreciate my private life being discussed by my superiors in front of my comrades. Especially not certain . . . *aspects* of it.' The combination of remembering Isaac and having the old man verbally pat her head like some pouting schoolgirl turned her stomach. The silence that followed was almost worse, though.

Agent Grosz changed the subject, giving Bianca a sidelong look of sympathy. 'Speaking of personnel shortages,' she said, 'the package arrived this morning.'

Bianca slumped back in her seat, idly wondering what had arrived and why they had decided to discuss requisitions at their weekly post-exercise meeting.

'He's in the compound?' Sturzer said.

'Wait. He?' Bianca asked, sitting back up.

'Yes,' Agent Grosz replied. 'Medical's checking him out right now, and I'm giving him the guided tour this evening. Get ready to meet your new team member.'

Chapter Five

Darius rubbed the sore spot on his arm with a wince. What exactly had all those injections been? The only explanation the doctors had given him was that they closely monitored everyone at the Nest for signs of illness. There were too many valuable personnel here—scientists, technicians, tacticians, and supervisors—to afford taking the slightest risk.

They'd told him all this while he ran on a treadmill with a dozen wires taped to his chest and arms, while he blew into a hose and made a rubber ball hover, and while he informed them of every risky behavior he'd ever engaged in. Then, when he was so exhausted he could barely move, they stuck him with something the orderly had called 'the vaccine to end all vaccines.'

Now he stood in a hallway waiting for Agent Grosz to come retrieve him. It was about a hundred feet of gray concrete, with no doors. The ceiling was low, fluorescent lights keeping the whole space at a uniform brightness. The doctors had hinted that they were underground, but he had no idea how *far* underground, or even what state they were under.

Was *this* what they'd snatched him from his life for? To run like a hamster and then stand around like a jerk? He took off down the hall, whistling over the faint buzzing of the lights. At the end, the hallway forked to the left and right into more stretches of featureless concrete hallways. He had barely taken ten steps when there was a soft *whoosh* somewhere behind him.

'Explore all you want. You won't find anything we don't want you to.'

He turned to see Agent Grosz, dressed in a suit identical to the one she had worn in Memphis. Darius wondered if she'd had it cleaned or if she owned several. Meanwhile, Darius was wearing white sneakers, black track pants, a gray T-shirt, and a black jacket, all made of some synthetic material he couldn't identify. They'd taken his clothes, muttering something about 'outside contaminants.'

'Fine. I'll just stand here for the rest of . . . however long you've got me. No skin off my butt.'

'Easy, kid,' she said. She pulled a remote out of her pocket and pressed one of a hundred tiny buttons on it. Shimmering seven-foot-high rectangles appeared on the concrete walls, spaced up and down the hallway. The shimmer turned into static, and then the static melted away to reveal solid steel doors. She stopped at a black wall panel with a confusing spiderweb of multicolored strands and opaque shapes. Hundreds of dots, each labeled in small type, flickered at different spots. It almost looked like a mall directory, but for a small city instead.

Agent Grosz's finger found a purple line and traced it to a series of purple squares. She stared for a moment and then seemed to find what she was looking for: two dots, one labeled LEON, the other labeled CONSTANCE.

'Where are we going, anyway?'

'I'm taking you to meet your teammates.' She resumed walking down the hall, stopping at a door that led into a small room with no other entrances. Darius assumed it was an elevator, though he was growing less and less comfortable making assumptions about this place as time went on. She pressed a series of numbers and letters on a panel near the door. 'This is where I first arrived too.'

'So you used to . . . ?' he began. Since he still wasn't all that clear on what *he* was going to be doing, he couldn't finish the question.

'Yes, I was a first-wave field agent,' she said, watching

the numbers on the panel light up as they moved. Darius could barely feel anything. 'Changelings, they called us then. The term has to do with Shakespeare, or fairies, maybe.'

'Don't you hate them?'

'Oberon?' She shrugged. 'At first. But I was a teenager. I hated everything, and I thought I knew everything. I always dreamed of joining the FBI after college anyway, so I guess I lucked out.'

'Couldn't you do that now? Or are we all slaves for life?'

'No,' she said. 'Field agents are free to do whatever they want after they turn twenty-three.'

'Yeah? What's to stop me from writing a tell-all book? What's to stop me from bargin' outta here and whistle-blowin' till I'm outta breath?'

She leveled a cold stare at him, saying nothing.

'What? You'll kill me?'

'I already told you, we have a *time machine*. Every single one of your plans to screw us over once you're out of here *will* fall apart twenty-four hours before its execution. Your life will turn into a never-ending succession of failures. We won't need to kill you, and everyone who hears you complain about the time-traveling secret agents out to ruin your life will think you're insane.'

'Something tells me that's happened before.'

She just smiled thinly without batting an eye. 'Anyway,

if you've got a talent, Oberon will almost always keep you on at the end of your term of service.'

'How nice. What if I'd had other plans?'

'Your girlfriend was leaving anyway,' Grosz said, as the elevator doors slid open. 'That's life. You learn to roll with it or, well, I think we both know the alternative.'

Darius balled his hands into fists. He followed Grosz out of the elevator and opened his mouth—but what he saw on the other side of the door stopped the words in his throat. He was standing on a catwalk above a yawning abyss, crisscrossed with more catwalks and platforms as far down as he could see. He looked up and saw that the same was true above him. He imagined this must be how astronauts felt when they left their ships while in orbit.

'Where are we?' he asked.

'The hub,' she said. 'Dormitory level, specifically. Try not to look down.'

'What is this place?'

'I told you, it's the hub.'

'Not where. *What?*'

'I don't know what it was before they set up Project Cronus down here, but parts of the complex are at least half a century old.'

'Project Cronus?' Darius asked. Curiosity had temporarily overtaken anger.

'You've had a long day,' Grosz said, 'and there are some

things you'll want to be rested and calm for. Let's just get you settled in.'

Rested and calm. The idea was tempting. It would be nice to let go, forget about the years he'd been on his own, forget about Zoe. It might feel good to just be told where to sleep and what to do. *No*, he decided just as quickly. They could boss him around, but they'd never have his consent.

'This is the main room of the field agent dormitory,' she said, leading him from the catwalks into a large room that was huge and airy, like an expansive loft apartment. A kitchen took up a third of the space, and a TV the size of a small movie theater screen hung on a wall facing a circle of overstuffed couches and chairs. Darius whistled and craned his neck back, looking up at the high, vaulted ceiling, its metal rafters draped with strings of red and blue lights.

'How many kids live here?'

'Five, including you.'

'Seems a little extravagant for five people.'

'There are perks to being a field agent. Oberon's pretty good about giving as much as it takes away.'

'I want the full Criterion Collection and a Sony Super 35-millimeter camera, then,' Darius said.

'Talk to me after you've saved the world, kid,' Grosz said, her cheeks pinching up in the faintest of smiles. 'Though I can't say the guys in Containment would be excited about people walking around with film equipment.'

She took him down a side hallway, stopping at one of the solid steel slabs that served as doors in the Nest. On it hung a black poster with an army of grim skeletons in World War I German helmets marching toward the viewer. LEAD POISONING, LIVE @ THE MAJESTIC was printed below in harsh white lettering. Speakers on the other side were blaring so loud that Darius could feel his teeth rattle.

'She's working,' Grosz said. 'She'll never hear if I knock.'

'She?'

'Constance Donnelly, codename Motorhead. One of the best wheelwomen I've ever met, and a prodigy with mechanics and field repairs.' She placed a hand on the door handle. 'You're going to want to cover your ears.'

Darius did as she said, but the blast of noise as the door swung open still hit him with an almost physical force. Agent Grosz ducked as though walking against a harsh wind and rushed over to an expensive-looking stack of stereo equipment on the far side of the room. She hit the power button, and the howling and thrashing was replaced by blessed silence. Darius followed her inside.

The room was huge, almost half the size of the main room, with a ceiling just as high. The walls were a motley collection of heavy metal concert posters, antique car parts and road signs, and collages from fashion magazines. A gigantic bed with a mountain of crumpled sheets and pillows tossed on the floor sat in one corner, and workbenches stood next to ornate dressers and armoires. There was a large vanity in one corner with what looked like a skull-shaped bass guitar leaning against it. The strangest thing about the room, though, was the harsh blue glow coming from a screened-off corner on the far side.

Darius was about to ask what the glow was when it stopped suddenly and the curtain was pulled aside, revealing a blond girl in black coveralls, her hair tied in a bun and covered by a bandana. She held a blowtorch in one hand and used the other to pull a pair of large, opaque goggles up to her forehead. Her eyes were large and shockingly blue.

'Why'd ya turn off my music?' She blinked once at Agent Grosz and then jumped when she noticed Darius. '*Oh!* The tour!'

She pulled off one of her welding gloves with her teeth and offered him a hand. He shook it tentatively and forced a smile.

'Heya!' she said, beaming and chipper in a way that Darius had never expected a metalhead to be. She was at least six feet tall. 'Name's Constance, but you probably already knew that. Pleasure to meet you.'

Darius had felt out of his element all evening, but people were something he could wrap his head around. He could charm people. He could read people. Provided, of course, they weren't gun-toting, humorless secret agents. He smiled and grasped Constance's hand as firmly as she grasped his.

'Darius Simms,' he said. 'Seems like you're quite the tinkerer.' He gestured to the blowtorch she still held.

'Oh, this?' she said, blushing. 'I'm just working on a costume for a side project, is all.'

'It's a long time till Halloween, last I checked.'

She blushed more and rubbed the nape of her neck. 'It's actually, uh, for my Aberrantart account. I do a lot of steampunk cosplay, and . . . I was working on a bronze top hat.'

'I don't really know what any of those things are,' Darius said. 'I'm sure it'll turn out great, though.'

She barked out an awkward laugh. 'Well-nice-to-meet-you-it's-been-great-see-you-around-back-to-work-bye!' she said, speaking too fast as she retreated behind the curtain. Agent Grosz walked back over to him, slowly shaking her head as she went.

'She seemed . . . nice,' Darius said as the door closed behind them.

'Constance Donnelly might be the last genuinely good person on the planet.'

'So what's behind door number two?' he asked as they came to another door.

'Leon Womack, codename Gygax. Field medic and communications technician. Likes to call himself a master hacker, and he's talented enough that nobody cares to argue.'

'Sounds like a good guy to know.'

'You'd think,' Grosz said. She opened the door and a low thrumming sound came out. This room was smaller than Constance's and lacking in personality. The twin bed was perfectly made. There was a small desk in one corner with a large high-definition computer monitor and a keyboard, and the rest of the wall space was taken up by two rows of server banks. A young man with a mop of brown hair was crouched at one of the servers, his back to Darius, working silently at something with a set of small pliers and screwdrivers. Grosz coughed to get his attention.

'I heard you outside,' he said flatly. 'I'll be with you in a moment.'

They stood there silently while he worked. Darius yawned and stretched his arms over his head, wondering when he would be shown to his own room.

Leon stood up after a few awkward moments and twisted, popping his back, then turned to greet them properly. He was thin, but not without muscle, and wore a black T-shirt that read THERE ARE 10 KINDS OF PEOPLE: THOSE WHO UNDERSTAND BINARY, AND THOSE WHO DON'T. He didn't smile but nodded to both of them.

'What can I help you with?'

'Just giving the tour,' Grosz said. 'Thought I'd introduce Darius here to everyone as soon as possible.'

'Okay, then,' Leon said. 'I'm Leon. It's been a pleasure,

but I'm very busy and I'm sure we'll both have lots of time to get tired of each other later.' He turned to Agent Grosz. 'Have you introduced him to Bianca yet?'

'No,' Grosz said. 'She's working out. He'll have to wait until tomorrow to meet her and Malik.'

'Probably for the best,' Leon said, eyeing Darius. 'Anyway, I need to get back to work. These upgrades don't make themselves.'

'Nice to meet you,' Darius said. He didn't go out of his way to make it sound too genuine.

'Mm-hmm,' Leon said, as he shuffled them out the door and closed it behind them.

'What a charmer,' Darius said.

'He has his reasons,' Grosz told him. 'Anyway, this is where the tour ends. There are a dozen unclaimed bedrooms in the dorm—pick whichever one you want. You'll find linens and blankets in a closet in the main room. The others will help you get in touch with the personnel necessary to get some personal effects. Any more questions?'

'Can I go home now?'

'This is home,' Agent Grosz said dispassionately. 'Good night, Mr. Simms.'

She walked down the hall and out into the hub, leaving Darius alone. He walked into the nearest empty bedroom, turned on the light for long enough to find the bed, and flopped down on it without even taking off his shoes.

He'd told himself he was going to cry once he was alone. Or that he was going to thrash and scream and beat his fists against the wall. Maybe both. He'd been holding something back all day, but now that he was finally by himself it felt pointless. The need to cry felt more like choking slowly. The anger was just a headache.

He closed his eyes, and nearly instantly he was enveloped in a dreamless sleep.

Chapter Six

Hungry and thirsty, his head pounding, Darius stumbled into the dorm's common room. It was empty except for a Middle Eastern-looking kid wearing black sweatpants and a gray tank top. Darius yawned and shuffled into the kitchen, scratching his side and blinking slowly.

'Long night?' the other guy said. He was lying on one of the couches with a bowl of Chex on his stomach. Darius, too tired to make decisions for himself, grumbled and poured the same kind of cereal.

'Yeah,' Darius said. 'Got a full medical exam and a guided tour. How big is this place, anyway?'

'The Nest? The original complex is a little under a square mile, with about twenty levels. The tunnels and satellite facilities stretch out a few miles in every direction, though.'

'Holy crap.' Darius poured too much milk into the cereal bowl and swore as he dabbed it up with a dish towel.

'Seems like overkill, right? Suffice it to say, we aren't the first group to use the place.'

Darius shuffled over to the couch, and the guy wordlessly sat up and patted the seat next to him.

'Thanks,' Darius said as he sat down. His eyes were still half closed, but he thought he heard Japanese coming from the television. 'Think that might be the friendliest reception I've had since I got here.'

'Who've you met so far?' the guy said.

'Constance,' Darius said through a mouthful of cereal, 'and Leon. Guy seemed like a jerk. What'd I do to get on his bad side?'

'Exist, I think.'

'Fantastic. Name's Darius, by the way.'

'Malik.'

'Cool. So what's your story, Malik?'

'Did anyone else give you theirs?'

'No.' Darius rubbed one eye and yawned. Malik was watching a black-and-white movie on their huge high-def screen. In it, a group of men in kimonos wielding samurai swords were defending a group of peasants from barbarians on horseback, but it looked like the men were having a hard time of it. One of them took a spear to the gut right as Darius started paying attention. 'I asked Grosz some stuff, but she seemed pretty guarded about it.'

'Well,' Malik said. 'How pleasant were the circumstances that led *you* here?'

'Point taken,' Darius said. 'I guess nobody wants to think about it.'

'Indeed. I might be the only person who's here of his own free will.'

'So you actually wanted this life?'

'No,' Malik said as he lifted another spoonful of cereal. 'But it was better than the alternative.' He put the spoon back in the bowl, its contents uneaten, and turned to Darius. 'Do you want some advice?'

Darius nodded.

'A wise man once said, "The basic difference between an ordinary man and a warrior is that a warrior takes everything as a challenge, while an ordinary man takes everything as a blessing or as a curse." So: How will you rise to this new challenge?'

'I'm not sure,' Darius said. He looked down into his bowl. His cereal was getting soggy. 'I'll have to think about it.'

'Very good. I would do most of that thinking later, though—I checked today's schedule, and it looks like you're late for your first training session with Bianca.'

Darius's heart sank into his stomach. 'Training? Nobody said anything about training.'

'Miss Grosz probably forgot to tell you, or Bianca neglected to tell her. Even here things fall through the cracks sometimes. At any rate, it is customary for team members to learn the basics of the skill sets held by all other members. I oversee everyone's drills at the rifle range, Constance does a weekly workshop on engine maintenance and field repair, Leon maintains a wiki on computer repair that I am almost certain nobody checks and trains us in basic first aid, and Bianca conducts her . . . exercises.'

'What's her specialty, though?' Darius said. 'If Constance is the grease monkey, Leon's your tech guy, and you're a sharpshooter, then what's she?'

'You'll see.' As Darius got up, Malik looked over his shoulder and said, 'Be careful.'

Darius glanced once more at the big screen before heading into his room to change. The last image he saw was a samurai in the rain, his chest full of arrows, howling as he fell to his knees.

Chapter Seven

Bianca's wrists throbbed and her knees burned, but she didn't care. *'What would you do without pain?'* Isaac had said to her once. She'd thought he was making fun of her.

She pivoted her hips, lunged forward, and flipped, using her hands to throw herself through space. Her current record for midair flips was three, but after the disappointment of the day before she had decided to break it. *One, two, three,* she counted as she spun, preparing for the fourth, but the sound of the gym door opening and the sudden appearance of a figure in her peripheral vision distracted her. The next thing she knew, she was bouncing along the mat like a rag doll.

She lay for a moment, trying not to groan, and then looked up. The new meat was standing a safe distance from her, his eyes open in surprise. *He's late.* She had forgotten that she was scheduled to train him, but the fact that *he* had apparently also forgotten irritated her.

'You okay?' the kid asked. 'That looked like it hurt.'

'Shut up,' Bianca said as she stood. She started to rub her shoulder but didn't want to embarrass herself. 'Darius, right? Where are your pads?'

Darius looked down. He wore a tank top, gym shorts, and white training shoes. 'What pads?'

'I left specific instructions on the schedule to attend our sessions in sparring pads.'

'I can go back and get them,' he said.

'Don't bother. We're already behind schedule.' She walked over to her gym bag and pulled out her own pads.

'You think you have what it takes?' Bianca asked. She circled him while she checked the lacing on her gloves. Darius shrugged, his hands in his pockets, sending a wave of annoyance up her spine.

'I know my way around a fight. Memphis ain't an easy city to live in when you're poor.'

'I'm sure your life's been really hard,' Bianca said sarcastically, remembering herself as a nine year old, dying of some unnamed disease her parents either couldn't afford or just didn't care enough to treat. That first night in the Nest she'd cried herself to sleep, lonelier than she'd ever felt. Then finally, for the first time, she opened herself to someone else—the only person she'd ever met who seemed to care for her without an ulterior motive. And look at how that had worked out. 'Let's see what you learned at the school of hard knocks. Try to hit me.' She dropped into a lazy defensive posture, but Darius didn't pull his hands out of his pockets.

'Are you sure?' he said. 'I didn't think I was, you know, supposed to hit—'

'If you finish that sentence, I'll beat you to death with your own arm,' Bianca said. 'And don't worry. You won't land a punch.'

'You're sure? I mean, will those pads protect you?'

'Oh, these aren't for my protection—now quit stalling and take a swing at me!'

Darius pulled his hands out of his pockets and inched toward her. He raised his fist in what he probably thought was a fighting posture. Once he was about three feet away he reached back and swung clumsily at her. She pivoted and drove her fist into the side of his rib cage.

'Is that the best you can do?' she said as he stumbled past her.

'N—' Darius began, but the word caught in his throat.

He closed his eyes, took a deep breath, and shook his head. 'No,' he said. 'I was holding back.'

Keep telling yourself that, Bianca thought.

'Why?'

'I was afraid I might hurt you.'

'I hope you learned your lesson,' she said.

He turned and barreled toward her, lowering his head and spreading his arms as he came. She spread her stance out to match him, but at the last minute leaped straight up. She landed lightly on the mat as his own momentum sent him sprawling out on the ground.

'You learned the wrong lesson,' she said.

'How do you figure?' he groaned as he rolled over onto his back and stood. 'I didn't hold anything back.'

'It doesn't matter *that* you were holding back. *Why* were you holding back? Why did you think you could hurt me?'

'Because you're a . . . because you're so much smaller than I am, I guess.'

He opened his mouth to say more, but instead swung at her head. She sidestepped it easily and jabbed him twice in quick succession, once in the stomach and once in the breastbone. While he was off balance, Bianca grabbed his upper arm, turned, and rolled his weight over her shoulder, leaving him once again in a heap on the floor.

'So how did I do that?' she said.

'I don't know,' he said between gasps. He took longer to

stand back up this time, and when he did, he immediately took a few steps away from her. She decided not to follow him this time—let him get his breath.

'Redirection of force,' Bianca said. 'You're bigger than me and stronger than me—it would be suicide for me to try to overpower you. I would lose. So, instead of facing you on your own terms, I face you on *my* terms.' She popped her neck and walked past Darius toward the center of the mat, delighting in the way he flinched as she neared him. 'Try and hit me again, but don't be stupid about it this time.'

'You enjoy this, don't you?'

'Follow your bliss,' she said, a smile crawling onto her face. 'Now stop stalling.'

He took a deep breath and ran at her again. He almost feinted her, leading with his right shoulder only to pivot and jab at her with his left arm. If Bianca had been a little slower he might have sunk his fist into her stomach, but instead she swiveled to the side, pushed his forearm away, and swept his legs out from under him. She put her hands on her hips, looked down at him, and nodded.

'That was an improvement,' she said.

'Thanks,' he coughed.

'So where was I? Redirection of force, right?'

Darius kicked at her legs. She hopped over the kick and landed with both of her heels on his knee, and he cried out in pain. She stood in place for a few seconds before giving him his leg back.

'For most of human history,' she said, 'your sixty-five extra pounds of muscle and bone meant you could carry heavier weapons and swing them harder. But in my world, killing depends more on hand-eye coordination than brute, physical force, and that's a world where almost all your natural advantages melt away.'

Darius stood up, putting his weight on his unhurt leg. He nodded, still panting heavily. 'I get it,' he said. 'I'm sold. You're tougher than me.'

She narrowed her eyes, and he stepped forward, bobbed with his right shoulder, ducked, and drove an uppercut with his left fist. Bianca pirouetted, pressed her back to Darius's, and jabbed her elbow into his kidney. He groaned and stumbled forward but, to his credit, didn't fall. Maybe he was tougher than she thought. Still, he was no Isaac.

The sudden appearance of her lost comrade in her thoughts opened her up to the usual barrage of memories. She clenched her fists and frowned, breathing heavily.

'The Night Witches,' she said. 'Ever heard of them?'

Darius shook his head.

'Female bomber pilots in the Soviet Air Force in World War II. Stalin's army was progressive for its time, but women still had to prove themselves at every turn and make do with the worst possible equipment. So these pilots were stuck with old single-propeller bombers left over from World War II. Their first flight was expected to be a suicide mission.'

'But it wasn't, of course.'

Bianca nodded, turning around. 'They were smart. They painted the undersides of their wings black, and when they got close to their targets they cut off their engines and glided, recklessly close to the ground. As far as the Germans could tell the night just exploded suddenly, without warning. So the—'

Darius's fist collided with the side of her head, sending her reeling. She blinked, trying to keep her balance. She barely stayed on her feet, but her vision swam. She touched her ear and brought her fingers up to check for blood. 'You punched me in the ear!'

'Sorry, I didn't know you were the only one who got to fight dirty.'

'You could've busted my eardrum!'

When Darius's eyes widened and he took a few steps back, she realized that she was screaming. She took low, even breaths. 'How did you do it?'

'It . . . it was simple,' he said. He squared his shoulders. 'You're pretty self-important. For real, you're probably the most arrogant person I ever met.'

'Go on,' she said. Her voice was deadpan now. She clenched her fists and brought them down to her side.

'I mean, all that business about redirection of force,

right? That's true with the mind, too. It's kind of what I do.'

'I see.' Anger twisted in her stomach.

'Where I come from, when you spend your life poor and on the outskirts, surrounded by cops and rich folks and a whole society that seems like it's dead set against you so much as getting by, you learn real fast that you can't win by running at that stuff head-on.'

'How harrowing your life must have been,' she said, narrowing her eyes.

'Whatever,' he snapped. 'Point is, you started throwing your weight around with that little speech, so I let you. You started believing I wasn't a threat at all, and that's when I became one.'

'You're not a threat.'

'Now *that's* a mindset that'll get you killed.'

'What do you know about dying?'

'I know I intend to last longer than that last chump did.'

A moment of electrified silence passed between them. Bianca's right eyebrow twitched.

'Say that again,' she said.

'I said I'm not goin' out early like that last sucker.'

Bianca was on him in a flash. She leaped and kicked him in his already hurt leg. He yelped and collapsed to the ground, where she fell on him, digging her forearm into his neck and pinning him. He swung at her, glancing her shoulder, but she barely felt it.

'That "chump's" name was Isaac. Remember it. Isaac. He was the best person I've ever met, and no one could ever replace him, let alone a skid mark like you. You're trash, and you'll be dead so fast I won't even remember your face.'

She kept him down for another few seconds, letting him squirm, letting him pull himself into even more painful contortions. The edge finally wore off her anger, and she let him go. He groaned and rolled onto his side.

'Next time you so much as think about mentioning your betters, remember what just happened.'

She sniffed and turned to see Constance and Malik standing in the door to the gymnasium. Constance's eyes were wide, and her hand was planted over her open mouth. Malik locked eyes with her and, after a long moment, slowly shook his head. He twisted his lips in an expression of mingled disgust and disappointment, and they walked away, leaving Bianca with nothing for company but Darius's moans.

Chapter Eight

'You know,' Darius said, 'the tour was great and all, but there's a lot y'all are still holding back.'

'Get used to it,' Leon said between gulps of milk. He had insisted he could handle Darius's lightning chili, and to his credit he was making a valiant attempt at hiding just how much pain he was in. Darius was pretty sore himself, and he was sporting a black eye after his training session with Bianca. But the team had wanted to welcome him all together over dinner, and he couldn't refuse the offer of company. It didn't dull the ache Zoe's absence left in his chest, or the guilt when he thought of his friends and few family members trying to figure out what had happened to him. But he had to move forward. This was his home now, like it or not. And he figured the best way to make himself at home here was to cook.

'Come on, man,' Darius said as he casually poured hot sauce into his chili. 'Don't hold out on me. This time travel business is *real*?'

'It is,' Malik said as he spooned sour cream into his bowl.

Darius raised his eyebrows. 'And?'

'I don't think you'd understand it,' Leon said.

'I know I don't,' Constance agreed.

'I mean, I don't need to know the math of it or anything, but I'm not stupid. Hit me with the theory.'

'Okay,' Leon said, pushing his bowl away, 'what do you want to know first?'

'Everything. I mean, explain to me how we go on a mission. Say something happens right now and we all get sent back—'

'As if you're anywhere *near* ready for the field,' Bianca muttered. An awkward silence followed, but eventually Darius picked up where he'd left off.

'So like I was saying, the sirens wail, the big man comes on the intercom, and off we go. What happens?'

'We head to the briefing room, pick up our gear, suit up, yada yada, all standard stuff. Once all the prep work is done, we head to the Junction Core, where we wait for mission control to activate the Chamber,' Leon said.

'You lost me,' Darius said. 'What were those last two things?'

'The Junction Core functions as a kind of gyroscope surrounded by six concentric particle accelerators, but instead of maintaining its orientation in space, its position is maintained in time. This stabilizes the Chamber, which is the largest zone of tachyon substitution made by scientists to date—and, by extension, the largest relativistic slip Oberon's engineers have been able to create so far.'

Darius blinked slowly and swallowed a bite of chili. 'I see,' he said.

'I don't!' Constance said. 'I think I understand it even less now.'

'I'm pretty sure he made most of that up,' Bianca said.

'You people.' Leon shook his head. 'If you'd stayed civilians I bet you'd be trying to decide between a degree in English and art history. I can only assume you want metaphors.'

The mention of college reminded Darius that none of the others were here of their own free will, either. He couldn't help wondering again what everyone's stories were. 'That'd be pretty helpful, yeah,' was all he said.

'Picture time as a train track in the middle of a void,' Leon said. 'We're on a train moving along the track.

Theoretically we can move any speed, forward or backward, right? Right.'

'That's it? Why didn't you just say that in the first place?'

'Don't interrupt! I'm not done. So the train can speed up, slow down, stop, move backward, whatever it needs to do, whatever the tracks and the terrain call for. There's a problem with this, though.'

'Stowaways?' Constance said.

Leon cast a glance at her that seemed almost worried and then shook his head. 'No, the problem is that no matter what the train does, it affects everyone on board equally. So you can seize one of the levers and throw it into reverse, but everyone goes with you. Same if you stop or speed up.'

'Seems like what you need,' Darius said, 'is another track.'

'More or less,' Leon said. 'If you can somehow build a track next to the first one, or gain access to one that was already there, nothing can really stop you from speeding up, slowing down, stopping, or even running in reverse relative to the train with everybody on it.'

'Wait a second,' Darius said, starting to understand. 'Are you implying that we could change the way the first train ran before we found the second track?'

'Are you asking if we could alter the flow of time throughout the universe?'

Darius nodded, his eyes wide.

'No, of course not. That would require titanic levels of energy that we're millennia away from learning to harness.'

'All right, cool, because that thought was horrifying and—'

'The effect is localized to our solar system.'

Darius felt something like his jaw dropping. Malik just smiled thinly and nodded.

'I hope you've figured out that the alternate track is the Junction Core and the train on the alternate track is the Chamber. Please tell me you gathered that much.' Leon frowned.

Darius nodded, still a little bit in shock. 'What are the rules?' he said after a moment.

'Come again?' Leon said through a mouthful of chili.

'The rules. Time travel always has rules, right? I assume there's one about us all being young.' At everyone's stare, he shrugged. 'Otherwise why would they recruit a bunch of teenagers to solve world disasters?'

'You're right.' Constance nodded, her cheeks rosy from the spicy food. 'The older the time traveler, the more damage the jump does to their body. Anyone older than their early thirties would probably die. That's why they retire us so early.'

'But don't think it'll be a breeze just because we're under the age threshold,' Malik warned. 'Especially those first few times, you'll still feel like you've been awake for a few days straight after a good working over by, well . . .' He stole a glance at Darius's fresh black eye.

'Nice simile,' Bianca said.

'I try.' Malik smiled.

'I don't know if that's true,' Constance argued. 'I usually just get a bit of a headache, and even that wears off after an hour.'

'That's because you're part Holstein,' Malik countered.

Constance threw a piece of cornbread at him, bouncing it off his shoulder. Leon frowned at the interruption and cleared his throat. 'Anyway, we were talking about rules. I guess there are only two: The first is that we can only travel backward in time, and then only twenty-four hours at the most. Think about how fast Earth spins, how fast it moves around the sun, and how fast the sun moves around the center of the galaxy, and so on. Our computers have to keep track of all that and more to avert any of a million disasters, and as it happens twenty-four hours is about the upper limit on our calculations for now. The second rule is that if you don't make it back into the Chamber before time catches up to the moment when you originally traveled back, you . . . well, we're not sure, really.'

'How are you not sure? Has it never happened?'

Leon swallowed and looked over at Bianca.

'Whatever,' she said. 'I don't care.'

'It's happened once,' Leon said. 'A few weeks before you were recruited.'

'Oh,' Darius said. 'Oh. I didn't know. I'm so sorry.'

'Forget it,' Bianca said. 'All you need to know is that you have to make it back on time. There's no coming home otherwise.'

'That seems like a pretty huge limitation,' Darius said. 'Even if our jurisdiction was just the continental US, it still takes, what, almost six hours to fly from New York to Los Angeles? And Agent Grosz told me we deal with worldwide threats.'

'We have access to some pretty impressive jets,' Constance said, an excited gleam in her eyes at the mention of her beloved machines. 'Travel times are still a problem, though.'

'That's the other reason the Chamber is so important,' Leon said. 'It has, as of our last update, nearly a hundred exits worldwide.'

'But the door's here in the facility, you said.'

'Right, but it's an extra-dimensional space. The Junction Core holds it stable, but it no more exists "inside" the facility than anywhere else. All you have to do is create a linked doorway, which is way easier than making a whole new Junction Core but still a logistical nightmare, and you can enter the Chamber from that door so long as it's still powered.'

Just then the light above the dorm entrance started flashing, and Major Sturzer's voice came over the intercom.

'The strike team will report to briefing room B immediately. There has been an incident.'

'Well,' Bianca said, pushing back her chair, 'looks like the lesson's over.'

Chapter Nine

Major Sturzer Stood at the bottom of the briefing room, a large lecture hall with a projector screen at the front. A handful of field agents, including Agent Grosz, were seated in the upper tiers, but the majority of the seats were empty. Bianca led everyone down to the second row and sat next to Director Spurling.

'Thank you for responding so quickly,' Sturzer said. 'I will not waste any time. We received the footage I am about to show you half an hour ago.' He pulled a remote out of his pocket and pressed a button.

A shifting pattern of light filled the background on the

screen, cast in harsh reds and blacks. It was a mixture of technological themes all whirling together—cogs spun, fed by churning steam engines, which in turn powered a series of blinking circuit boards lined with vacuum tubes like watching eyes. Over a century of industrialization and mechanization danced and spun and sparked. After a few seconds, Darius realized that it formed a pattern, a kind of nautilus spiral or fractal. At its center, almost impossible to see against the background, was the silhouette of a man sitting in a plain office chair.

Everyone in the briefing room passed glances back and forth, whispering to one another in hushed tones. Bianca seemed to be the only person keeping silent.

'Let me begin by saying that I'm not entirely sure why I'm bothering with this,' a smooth, calculated voice intoned. Though Darius couldn't see him speaking, he could tell it belonged to the shaded man on the screen. 'It's not like anyone has ever listened before. And I'm sorry to say, the odds of your continued survival if you're seeing this are not terribly high.'

The man's hand rose and the lights above him went up, revealing a tall, well-muscled figure in his late twenties, or maybe early thirties. His hair was dirty blond and looked like it might have been stylishly cut a month or two previously, but was now haphazardly mussed. His rumpled gray suit looked expensive, his tie loosened. The dark circles under his eyes were accentuated by the deep shadows cast from the overhead light. His mouth was pulled into a straight line.

'Please pardon my appearance,' he continued. 'Things around here have been busy lately, the last week especially so. But it should be worth it. I hope it will be worth it.' He leaned forward, clasping his hands together. 'We're talking about the end of an age—the erasure of a mistake.

'Things have gone unchecked for too long. We, as a species, have gone unchecked for too long. We have consumed without discipline and expanded without a care, and to what purpose? So that we might live longer? What's the point of a longer life spent in idle drudgery and mindless, apocalyptic consumption? And that's just for those of you lucky enough to live in the richer parts of the First World. For everyone else, hunger, disease, and slavery are as constant now as they were three thousand years ago. You're destroying the world in the name of your own sloth and avarice.

'There was a time when the night, and the wilderness, and all the horrors those entailed, played the role of the guiding hand of our parent. But we outgrew our mother's ability to chastise us far too quickly. We are still, in all the ways I can see, children, and you know what they say: Spare the rod, spoil the child. And so here we find ourselves, and I sincerely want you to know that what is about to happen hurts me as much as it hurts you.'

The screen went black immediately. Motion and sound erupted to either side of Darius.

'That's not all,' Sturzer said, calling the group to order. 'A satellite in orbit above North America recorded the following series of images approximately five minutes after the video feed ended.' He raised the remote and pressed a button, revealing a large, crisp satellite image of New York City from above. Darius sucked in a breath and dug his fingernails into his palms.

Zoe. She was down there somewhere.

Click. The next image was almost identical, except for a bright pinpoint of blue light situated in the center of Manhattan. The lights were out in a radius around the blue dot, where they had been numerous and bright before.

Click. Lines of blue luminescence had begun to spread out from the central point. It looked as though they were following the streets, but it was impossible to tell as the lights had now gone out in almost half the city. Darius imagined Zoe standing on one of those streets. Though he had no idea what the blue light meant, his throat tightened.

Click. The lines had begun to bleed into one another, suffusing the entire city in a fuzzy blue glow. Arcs of energy flowed from line to line like a gigantic Tesla coil. The blue energy was the only light source remaining in the image.

Click. The light was gone, leaving New York City utterly dark. Somewhere in the blackness was the girl he loved.

'It took almost an hour after the event for the reports to reach us,' Sturzer said after a moment, 'as every electronic device within the city was completely, irrevocably disabled. The latest reports indicate that the power infrastructure of New York City and most of the surrounding sprawl has been annihilated, and that the grid for the entire Northeast has been crippled.'

'Casualties?' Director Spurling said.

'No way of knowing,' Agent Grosz said from the tier above and behind Darius. 'Our short-term projections run anywhere from the high thousands to the tens of thousands, mostly from car accidents, planes falling out of the sky, and the like.'

'Long-term?'

'Eight million people live in New York City alone, sir. How many of those are trapped in subway cars? How many are trapped in elevators? How long do you think hospital generators are going to hold out? And that's just in the next few *days*. FEMA had enough trouble getting food and water into New Orleans after Katrina, and those conditions were ideal next to what we're looking at here, considering the few bridges and the dense urban development. People are going to dehydrate, and they're going to starve, and they're going to get sick. And once they start to realize that there's limited food, water, and medicine, they're going to start fighting one another.'

'Nonsense,' Spurling said. 'These aren't animals, they're people—*Americans*, for crying out loud!'

'This is just off the top of my head, sir. I have a whole notebook here, but I hope you get the idea. You're looking at a death toll in the millions if we don't act.'

Director Spurling leaned back and ran his hand down his face, contorting his features in frustration. 'All right. What do we know about the man in the video?'

'Not much,' Major Sturzer said. 'Apparently he calls himself Ludd.'

'What was that blue light?' Darius choked out. He could barely think, haunted by images of Zoe under the wreckage of a fallen plane, Zoe dying in a hospital without power, Zoe being killed by a crazy, nightmarish mob.

Major Sturzer frowned. 'At first we assumed it was some kind of EMP. However, our scientists can't identify the sort of weapon that would cause that blue light, or if it's even a weapon at all. We can only assume it's some kind of bomb. Whatever it is, we've narrowed down the point of origin for the blast, but we haven't been able to pinpoint it.'

'So we're being sent out?' Malik said.

The director glanced at the young man, scratched his chin, and finally nodded. 'I suppose we have no choice,' he said. He clicked again, and a clear satellite image of Manhattan during the day appeared. He pointed at a spot at the tip of the island. 'This is the closest ingress we have in Manhattan, near Battery Park. You will need to use the remote locators to pinpoint the device, which can only be done from a height of over a hundred meters. You should be able to find plenty of suitable buildings in Manhattan. From there, it will be up to you to find the device and determine a way to disarm it.'

'Resistance?' Bianca said.

'Unknown.'

'I guess you want the device, too, right?' Leon said.

'It has been deemed too dangerous for introduction into the Chamber,' Sturzer said. 'If at all possible, however, you are to hide it securely so that a team can retrieve it later.' He turned and locked eyes with Bianca. 'That is all. Have your team ready within the hour and report to Agent Grosz outside the Chamber.'

Bianca stood and saluted.

'Dismissed,' Director Spurling said. He returned his eyes to the screen, lacing his fingers on the table. Bianca turned and indicated for the others to follow her. Darius stood, trying to stop his limbs from shaking. 'Oh, and Miss Albert?' he said. She turned. The others walked past her and out into the hall, but Darius lingered for a moment, curious. 'I know that things have been rough for you of late, but I have every confidence that you will succeed.'

'Thank you, sir,' she said.

Darius didn't wait for the end of the exchange. He made

his way to the armory, grabbed one of the gear packs, and headed into the boys' dressing room as Leon was leaving. The smaller boy gave him an odd look, but Darius glowered and shoved past him. Malik was just finishing getting dressed. He wore a pair of jeans with various holsters and ammunition pouches stitched in so that a passing observer would never notice them. Above that was a light-blue T-shirt with the words YOU GIVE LOVE A BAD NAME across the chest in dark pink. A bulletproof vest was visible through the thin material, which Malik was in the process of covering with a plaid overshirt. He looked up as Darius entered and blinked.

'Uh,' he said. 'Hi.'

Darius didn't acknowledge him. He replaced his slacks with a pair of dark gray trousers similar to Malik's, with room for a sidearm, five extra clips of ammunition, a stun grenade, and a fragmentation grenade. Next, he clipped his own Kevlar vest into place and rebuttoned his dress shirt over that. There was a dark gray vest in the bag, matching his pants, with concealed pockets on the inside containing a knife, a stunner, and a small radio.

'She's not going to let you come with us,' Malik said. He shouldered a rifle that was almost as tall as he was.

'I'm ready,' Darius said, not looking up as he clasped his belt.

'Be that as it may, she won't let you.'

'She can't stop me.'

'Of course she can,' Malik said. 'Or have you not looked in a mirror today?'

Darius touched his bruised eye and scowled. Malik crossed the room and put a hand on his shoulder. He leaned in close, a look of concern on his face.

'I know this looks bad, but it's not the worst we've ever faced.'

Darius wanted to say, 'I don't care if *you* need me,' but something told him that if he said anything about Zoe, about being emotionally involved, there would be zero chance of going. He had to be there, though. He had to make sure she was safe.

He shrugged and started walking past Malik. 'This is my life now,' he muttered. 'Might as well get a head start.'

Bianca was standing in the armory, waiting for him as he left the dressing room. Her hair was pulled up into a ponytail, and she wore a stylishly oversize white T-shirt with a fanged, purple-skinned, six-armed woman on the front. A pair of skintight black capris concealed a knife sheath on one hip.

'No,' she said. Her scowl could have curdled milk.

'Yes,' Darius said. He moved to pass her, but she stood in his way.

'You'll get killed.'

'Like you care.'

'Fine. You'll get *us* killed.'

His eyes narrowed to slits. This girl had made his life twice as miserable as it needed to be since he'd arrived, and this was the last straw. He drew his pistol and pointed it at her, trying to keep his hand from shaking.

'I'm coming,' he said. 'Or nobody is.'

Her eyes widened, but she didn't look nearly as surprised or afraid as Darius would have liked. She was too relaxed, and it occurred to Darius that she should have been able to draw at least as fast as him, or disarm him with some martial arts move. Instead she just stood there, biting her lower lip as though she was thinking. Finally she stepped forward and, in a flash, yanked the pistol out of his grip. She flipped a switch on the side and handed it back to him. 'You forgot to turn off the safety.' She gave him one last, long look. 'You really want to go to New York, and that drive's an asset to any mission. But don't be so blinded by your emotions that you do something stupid. This isn't practice anymore.'

Bianca turned and walked away from him. He let out a long breath and holstered his weapon. She stopped at the door and turned, giving him an oddly empathetic look.

'Whoever she is,' she said, 'I hope she's worth it.'

Chapter Ten

The Junction Core was a gigantic sphere made out of a mesh of crisscrossed metal bars. A series of catwalks led to the very center, joining at a burnished metal cube about fifteen feet in length on all sides. Darius and the others stood on the edge, just off one of the catwalks. A series of glowing rings could be seen outside the mesh—he guessed they were the particle accelerators. A thrumming sound filled the air like a gigantic heartbeat. The lights glowed and darkened in the rings. Each time light passed through the portion of one of the rings closest to the team, their hair stood on end as though being attracted by static electricity.

There was a *whoosh* behind them, and they turned to see Agent Grosz walking into the Core. She stepped onto the nearest catwalk and headed toward the Chamber. Darius and the others followed, trying not to look down.

'You heard the briefing,' she said. 'This should be pretty straightforward. Don't draw attention to yourselves. Get in. Get out. Your mission is to disarm whatever that device is—there are other people whose job it is to hunt down the bad guy, so don't do anything stupid.'

'I never knew you cared,' Malik said.

Darius watched as Agent Grosz keyed a long combination into a blue glowing pad next to a seam in the wall of the Chamber.

'Is that a security code?' Darius said.

'Coordinates,' Leon said. 'What exists inside this metal cube right now is, technically speaking, nothing. Each of the doors has a pad like that outside it somewhere—you key in the location of the door and current time, and that's what opens it.'

'How do you know the codes?' Darius said.

'*You* don't,' Agent Grosz said. 'Your tech specialist does and, in a pinch, op support does. But calling us is risky.'

'Why's that?'

Agent Grosz finished keying in the numbers, and the seam glowed light blue. Then, like a picture loading on a slow connection, the metal within the seam disappeared from top to bottom, revealing a completely empty room inside with eggshell walls, ceiling, and floor.

'Ever heard the word *paradox*?' she said as she walked into the Chamber. She turned around, arms clasped behind her back, and waited as the rest of the team filed in.

'I think so,' Darius said. He was the last to enter. 'In a sci-fi movie. It's like when you kill your own grandfather before he has a chance to meet your grandma, right?'

'It's more or less like that.' Agent Grosz pulled out an iPhone-like device and checked a few files, speaking to him absentmindedly. 'But it doesn't need to be that dramatic. Anything you do that negates the conditions that caused the action can cause a paradox.'

'What's the problem with that, though?'

'The problem with a paradox,' she said, 'is that it literally can't happen. Except that now that we have the technology you're standing in, it can.'

'How can it be possible and impossible for something to happen, all at once?'

'We're not sure,' Agent Grosz said, 'but we're not taking any risks. My presence here is about as far as we're willing to push it.'

'How do you mean?'

'God,' Bianca said. 'Do you never stop asking questions? Some of us like a little quiet before we put our lives at risk.'

'Ease off him,' Agent Grosz said. She turned back to

Darius. 'I'm on paradox duty. I've got all the information relevant to this mission on my assistant here.' She indicated the device in her hands. 'I show up, hand off the information to a guard, and report to an isolation chamber. The higher-ups go over the intel, and then they put the entire compound on lockdown—not so much as a photon gets in or out. Then, exactly twenty-four hours after I arrive, the past versions of yourselves are sent back to accomplish the same mission you will have ideally just completed.'

'That's a little disappointing,' Darius said.

'How do you figure?'

'I was kind of hoping to meet myself.'

'A universe blasted out of existence through vanity,' Malik said. 'The ancient dramatists would be proud, I think.'

Just then, Major Sturzer's voice filled the room. 'Everyone ready?' Darius looked around, but he didn't see a speaker or an intercom.

Agent Grosz looked at everyone in turn, and they nodded. Darius did as well, although he wasn't sure if he was truly ready or not. Agent Grosz pressed a button on her assistant and said, 'Engage.'

Darius immediately felt weightless. A loud *thrummmmm* vibrated deep inside his chest. An intense pressure hit his body, like the centrifugal force on a carnival ride, but instead of being pulled backward, every molecule of Darius's body felt like it was being pulled inward. The feeling was more nauseating than painful. His eyes seemed to be watering, blurring his vision, but when he rubbed them, there was no moisture. It was difficult to see, but Agent Grosz seemed to be taking it the hardest. The smear of her figure was half the height it should have been; she was probably kneeling and holding her stomach.

Then, suddenly, it was over. The weight of his body returned to his feet, his vision was clear, and the only after-effects were the same as a mild cold: His skin was a little tender, and his balance was off just a touch. Agent Grosz, on the other hand, was leaning against the back wall, arms wrapped tightly around her midsection, eyes closed, panting. Darius started to ask if she was okay, but she held up a hand.

'Get out. Find out what caused the explosion. Get to the nearest door. I have to do this again, and I'd like to get it out of the way as quickly as possible.'

One of the walls hissed, and a seam started to open in it. Was this the same wall as before? Darius was having a hard time remembering. His sense of direction was off. As the door finished scrolling down, he was met with a skyline, a smell, and a background noise of honking horns and muttering voices.

He headed out the door and found himself standing on a rooftop. New York Harbor was visible through the tall buildings.

'All right,' Bianca said, as they all turned and stood at attention. 'This is deadly serious, and we're a man down.' She looked flatly at Darius. 'No offense.'

Darius shrugged. The door slid closed behind Bianca, leaving only a bare wall with a number pad bolted on at about chest height. His eyes were drawn to a red dot. At first he thought it was his imagination, but as he looked closer Darius was certain that a pinpoint was traveling up Bianca's body. 'Bianca?'

'That's Captain Albert to you,' she said as she did a final check on her sidearm.

'No,' Darius said, 'you don't understand, there's—'

'No, *you* don't understand,' Bianca said as she holstered her pistol. '*I'm* in charge here, and—'

The dot had drifted up to her chest. There was no time to argue. Darius barreled into Bianca, wrapping his arms around her midsection, and drove her to the ground.

'Get off me!' she shrieked, but was drowned out by the sound of a high-powered rifle shot.

'Everyone down!' Darius shouted. The rest of the team hardly needed the instruction. Bianca's face had gone ghost white. 'I'm sorry,' he said, still pinning her.

'No,' Bianca said. 'Um. Thank you.'

They stared at each other for a few seconds before Darius tried to pick himself up. Bianca grabbed him and pulled him close.

'No!' she said. 'The sniper is still out there! We have to get to the maintenance door and—what's that?' She turned and pointed, first at Malik, then at the nearby door. Malik crawled over and listened for a moment. He turned to them with his eyes wide.

'Footsteps. Half a dozen at least,' he said. 'We've got company.'

Bianca pushed Darius off and leaned up on her elbows, catching Malik's eye. 'Did you get the direction on that bullet?'

Malik nodded once and shouldered his rifle. He held up one hand with three fingers raised, and Bianca did the same in response. He mouthed, *Three,* at her, and they counted off on their fingers in unison. As they did so, the footsteps in the stairwell grew louder.

'Go!' Bianca said.

Darius unholstered his weapon, remembering to disengage the safety this time. Bianca rolled once and came up at a crouching run, headed straight for the door. Another sniper shot rang out as she did so. Malik jumped up as she passed him, raised his rifle, and fired. There was no time to see if he had hit his mark.

The maintenance door opened a crack. Bianca pivoted to the side, swung it open, and jammed her knife into the stomach of the first man. He wore strange, futuristic-looking bright-white armor of overlapping vinyl and plastic plates.

As the first man fell, two more ran up to replace him. Bianca stood and shot her foot into the air, kicking above her head. Her heel collided with the chin of the man on the right, sending him hurtling back down the stairs. A second man drew a bead on her faster than she could respond. Darius pulled the trigger once, twice, three times, hoping against hope that he didn't miss and hit Bianca. A few seconds later, the final figure was falling into a heap as three spots of red grew on his chest and stomach.

'You're welcome,' Darius said. Bianca turned around, raised an eyebrow, and nodded.

The team drew closer to examine the armor. The helmets were perfectly smooth and white, with no markings other than a black design on the faceplate. A horizontal line ran where the bridge of the nose would be, with a capital I along the nose and goggle lenses in the shapes of thick Xs over the eyes. Another black line curved away from the left eye, rising in a repetition of the pattern toward what Darius could only assume was some kind of comm antenna.

'Leon,' Bianca said. 'Grab one of those helmets, and let's head out.'

Leon pulled off the helmet of the man Darius had shot. Darius wasn't sure what he had expected their assailant to look like, but the plain twenty-something male staring, unblinking, up into the sky wasn't it.

Malik looked up as a final shot rang out. He flinched as

a red cloud exploded from his thigh, and tumbled onto the ground.

Bianca leaped toward him. Darius was right beside her as she braced Malik against her shoulder, helping her lift their injured comrade. They dragged him as fast as they could, taking cover inside the stairwell. They all huddled down and, at least for a moment, they were safe and out of sight. Leon immediately began examining Malik's leg.

'Is he going to be all right?' Darius said. His breath was coming in gasps, and he couldn't stop his hands from shaking.

'I don't know,' Leon said. 'I need to get someplace where I can see the wound.'

They all sat back on their heels, breathing the still air of the stairwell, listening.

Constance finally broke the tense silence. 'I'll be the first to say it: They knew where we were going to be.'

Darius's stomach knotted up. 'That's impossible,' he said. Something about the way the team looked at one another, eyes wide and mouths pulled tight, told him they had the same thought. 'Right?'

Nobody responded.

Leon hooked the assailant's helmet up to his computer and began furiously typing. He shook his head and frowned.

'Any idea what we're dealing with?' Bianca said.

'None,' Leon said. 'Their systems are sophisticated. The only other place I've seen encryption this tight is, well . . .'

'Let me guess,' Bianca said. 'Back at the compound?'

He nodded.

Darius looked back and forth between them. 'So even though we traveled back in time, sophisticated soldiers with technology similar to our own knew exactly where we were going to be, and when.' He was met with resigned silence. His eyes flicked back to the growing red stain on Malik's pant leg. 'Where do we go from here?'

The confused, worried look on Bianca's face scared him more than anything. 'I don't know.'

'You two take a sightseeing tour,' Leon said. He wiped the blood off his hands and handed Bianca his handheld computer. 'You know I'll kill you myself if you lose this, right?'

She nodded.

'The locating script for the device is already pulled up,' Leon said. He nodded to Constance, and together they moved Malik to an out-of-sight area of the rooftop, between a wall and a large air-conditioning unit. Leon grunted and continued, 'Like Major Sturzer said, there's too much ground interference, so you'll need to get higher than most of the rest of the buildings.'

'Great,' Darius said, taking in the city's suddenly ominous skyline. 'That should be easy.'

Chapter Eleven

23:00 remaining

The flickering fluorescent lights made the subway station seem even more subterranean—and for some reason, they made Bianca nervous. Funny, how she'd lived almost her whole life underground, but it had never bothered her like this did. Maybe it was just the crowds getting to her. The sheer thought of so many strangers made her mouth feel dry. She licked her lips and ran a finger along a promising route on the subway map.

'Why are we taking the subway?' Darius said. 'Couldn't

we just walk to the Empire State Building?'

The sight of him leaning casually against the wall, his hands in his pockets, irritated Bianca no end. If anything, Darius seemed *more* relaxed underground, surrounded by masses of people.

'Not safe,' Bianca said. 'There could be gunmen on a rooftop, or hanging out any of the thousands of windows we'd pass on the way.'

'Hadn't thought of that,' Darius said.

'Which is why I'm in charge.'

'Whatever you say.' Darius rolled his eyes and turned away from Bianca. 'Subway's the best option anyway, now that I think about it.'

'What's that supposed to mean?' She glared at him.

'You're conspicuous,' he said without turning to face her. 'You're like a tourist but worse.'

'*I'm* like a tourist?' Bianca said. 'How many times did you leave . . . wherever it is you're from?'

'Memphis,' Darius said. 'And a few times, in fact.' He scratched his chin and studied the map, dragging one finger along a route that interested him. 'It's not about where you're from or where you've been, though. It's all in the way you carry yourself. You gotta look like you're supposed to be wherever you are. You gotta pretend you're bored even if you're sweating through your shirt.'

Bianca wanted to remind Darius angrily that no level of cool could stop bullets—but she thought of all the friends she'd never gotten to make, all the dances she'd never attended, and felt heat rise to her cheeks. 'So I'm . . . whatever. Dorky, I guess. It doesn't affect our mission.'

'It does if you've got people after you who know *where* you are but maybe not *what* you look like. Folks who are looking for anything out of the ordinary.'

A mechanical screeching noise filled the station. Dozens of people shuffled up to the platform as the train rattled in from the tunnel, leaving Darius and Bianca standing by themselves, their only other company a woman talking softly on her cell phone. Darius turned to face Bianca again and gave an almost imperceptible nod toward the woman. She was tall and hard-featured, wearing what looked like white-and-black leather motorcycle padding. Bianca hadn't noticed her before, but something about the woman made her skin crawl.

'You're sure?' Bianca said. Her whole body seemed to grow a few degrees cooler as adrenaline shot through her brain, washing away her anxieties, her fears, even her annoyance with Darius. This was why she kept hurling herself at danger, she thought. This feeling of alertness filled her up, sharpened her senses, leaving her with nothing to worry about except the perfect, clean blade's edge of the present. She cracked her neck and moved her hand closer to her hidden knife.

Darius nodded. 'Her outfit has the same colors as the armor of the guy I killed, and in a similar pattern. Plus—there's no cell phone reception down here.' He hunched his shoulders and loped toward the train, easily blending into the crowds as they gathered near the doors.

Bianca caught up to him, sparing the woman in the leather jacket one last glance. Her eyes darted away just as Bianca turned. Had she been watching? Bianca's hands flexed and reached for her knife, to check that it was there.

'Is she moving?' Darius said.

'No.'

'Okay, well, this is our train.'

Bianca read the sign above the door and scowled. 'But this is going east!'

'To Brooklyn, yeah,' Darius said softly, motioning for her to be quiet. 'We won't be on it for long.'

'You have a plan, then. What is it?'

'There's no time!' He started off toward the door.

'Hold on,' Bianca said, grabbing his arm. 'We're don't have time for any detours. And don't forget that I'm in charge, so I make the rules.'

Darius tried to pull away, but Bianca's grip was stronger. He glared at her, then looked over her shoulder. 'She's moving toward us now,' he said, his voice low, 'and reaching in her jacket for something. I'm pretty sure it's not a love note.'

'Okay, fine,' Bianca said. She pushed past Darius and slipped onto the middle car, barely managing to squeeze her way between a large man in a suit and a bored-looking nurse. Darius appeared suddenly beside her, gliding easily through the crowd with small, tiny pushes and timed slides, giving people a wry grin and a wink whenever they noticed him. She tried to reply in kind, but the press of bodies made her heart beat so fast she could feel her pulse in the back of her neck. She took a few slow, deep breaths to calm herself and closed her eyes, pretending she was alone in a dark room.

'I can see why they put you in charge,' he said, pointedly not looking at her. He kept his back slightly turned so that they would look like strangers to a casual observer.

'Shut up,' she said. She opened her eyes, feeling a little more centered, and craned to try to see above the crowd. 'You're taller than me. Is she coming?'

'I can't see her on the platform. She must have gotten on a different car.'

'We need a new plan,' Bianca said. She felt under her voluminous T-shirt for the bulge of her knife and pulled it out of its sheath, keeping it hidden under the cloth. 'I say we go over to the next car, kill her, and disappear in the chaos before the cops arrive.' A few of the commuters sitting around her shifted uncomfortably and looked away. She ignored them.

'We can't do that,' Darius said. 'Remember our timetable? We're headed in the wrong direction, which means we'll need to take the train to get back. There's no way you can do your thing without everybody on the car seeing, and how easy will it be to catch another train then? Trust me. Like I said, I have a plan.'

A door opened at the other end of the car.

'What was that?' Bianca said. 'I can't see! Was that a door? Can people move between cars while the train's moving?'

'I'm not sure.' Darius stood up higher, trying to look over the crowd. 'It's probably against the rules, but once you're up to mass murder I guess safety regulations aren't much of a concern. We ought to—' His eyes widened.

A black-and-white figure came into Bianca's peripheral vision, and Darius bolted, disappearing into the crowd. Metal glinted, and the man in the business suit gasped. Did the woman have a gun? There was no time to find out. Bianca reached out, grabbed the woman's wrist, pinned it to her sternum, and kicked her right leg away, forcing her to stumble forward. This left the woman leaning with her face inches from Bianca's, looking for all the world as though they were trying to have a private conversation. Someone would have to be situated directly between them to notice the painful way the woman's arm was twisted, and the way that twist made her own gun point up at her.

'Go ahead,' the woman said softly. 'Pull the trigger.'

Bianca took in the woman's features. She was hard and lean, but she looked more like a college student than a hired mercenary. The woman twisted her head to the side and smiled.

'I have other plans,' Bianca said.

'You can't stop me,' the woman hissed. 'I'm going to get my gun free as soon as the train stops, and then I'm going to kill you, and then I'm going to find your partner and kill him, too.'

'You know why I didn't slit your throat just now?' Bianca whispered into the woman's ear. 'Because it would have been *inconvenient*.'

The woman licked her lips and flared her nostrils, her eyes darting quickly back and forth. *She's nervous,* Bianca thought. There was a sheen of sweat on the woman's forehead, and her pupils were dilated. Bianca realized the woman probably could have shot her and Darius on the platform, but she hadn't done it. She had hesitated.

'This is your first time,' Bianca said slowly.

'What?'

'You could still walk away. Go back to your family, or school, or whatever.' *Or,* Bianca thought, *you could take the gun back, pull the trigger, and become just like me.*

The train screeched, and she felt her weight lean to the left as they pulled into the next station. The woman used the opportunity to jerk her hand forward, pushing the gun barrel into Bianca's ribs.

'Nice try, princess,' the woman said softly. 'But I don't scare that easily.'

Bianca cried out and grabbed at the woman's hands, trying to find a way to escape, but now that she had the leverage the woman was surprisingly strong. People were turning to look at them. *So much for being inconspicuous*, Bianca thought. All these strangers were going to see her die. The sticky, paralyzing ball of terror deep in her stomach twisted into a surprisingly acute sense of shame. The woman pressed her forehead into Bianca's and laughed.

'I believe in something far greater than myself. While you, you're just a little mercenary. I wouldn't be so superior if I were you.'

'My shoe!' a woman screamed from across the train. 'You horrible little hooligan!'

Bianca closed her eyes and braced herself, waiting for the gunshot—but at that moment, a white high-heeled shoe spun over the crowd and bounced off the side of the woman's head. The woman cursed and grabbed her temple, giving Bianca a split second to slip away. She drove through the crowd like a freight train through a herd of cattle, kicking and shoving anyone stupid or slow enough to stand in her way. Some inward part of Bianca was cringing at the terrible mission conduct, but she couldn't think about that now. She had to get off the subway car.

Dimly, she realized that no one was even reacting to

her aggressive behavior: They were all distracted by a scene at the other end of the car. And Bianca only knew one person manipulative enough to draw the attention of a crowd this size, and keep it. She shoved a delivery guy out of the way and found Darius, huddled with his hands over his head in the center of a ring of people as an elderly woman thrashed him with her handbag. Bianca suppressed a smile when she noticed the woman's single naked foot.

'A little help?' Darius said. Bianca wanted to savor the image for another minute, but she knew their attacker was still behind them. She grabbed Darius by the elbow and apologized to the older woman, catching a few hits from the purse herself. They ran out onto the platform together a few seconds before the doors closed again.

'You disappeared,' Bianca said accusingly.

'I hid!' Darius exclaimed. 'She had a gun!'

They both turned at the sound of a muffled thumping from behind them. The woman was hammering against a window with the butt of her gun, screaming at them as the train started carrying her away. The last thing Bianca saw before she disappeared into the tunnels was a crowd of angry-looking men closing in from behind, poised to wrestle the weapon away from her.

'Quick thinking, with the shoe,' Bianca said.

'I do some of my best work with rich old women,' Darius

replied with a smile. 'Bet the lady in the jacket feels pretty stupid right about now.'

'We can't count on her friends being as gullible, though.'

'Yeah,' Darius agreed. 'They've been waiting for us everywhere else so far. I'd almost be disappointed if they didn't know where we were actually headed.'

Another train pulled in on the opposite platform and they boarded, Bianca doing her best to copy Darius's casual posture. She rolled her shoulders forward and drifted her eyes into the middle distance while still doing her best to keep an eye on what was happening around her.

'She'll try to follow us, you know, once she's off that train,' Darius said.

Bianca winced. 'I hope not.'

'She was that dangerous, huh?'

'No. I could have slaughtered her.'

'But you didn't.'

Bianca didn't have anything to say to that, so she just turned and watched as the lights on the tunnel wall streaked into one long, glowing line.

Chapter Twelve

22:00 remaining

Darius had seen the Empire State Building before, on television and in movies. He vaguely remembered an aunt having a model of it above her toilet when he'd been a little kid. Here, though, in real life, it was so much bigger than it had ever seemed on screen. But he resisted the urge to stand there looking up at it. His father used to say that you could always tell a small-town tourist by following their eyes. Locals looked down.

'See the scaffolding?' Bianca said. There was a tremendous

wind blowing down the street, channeled by the rows of tall buildings that formed a sharp wind tunnel. It whipped Bianca's shoulder-length hair into a frenzied mane and blew her baggy shirt in a pattern that made Darius yearn for his camera. She turned to him and frowned, and he realized he'd been staring.

'Sorry,' he said, 'I was just thinking about something.'

'Whatever.' Bianca rolled her eyes. 'I was saying, it looks like they're doing some kind of maintenance on the upper floors.'

'Which is . . . good?'

'It's interesting. I was hoping we could just take the tour, but the mission goes on.'

She crossed the street and he followed. His mind kept drifting back to her hair, twirling in the breeze, and the way her shirt flattened against her side. He tried bringing his mind back to Zoe, but all he could see was Zoe crushed under a pile of rubble, or Zoe sick in a hospital without medicine or power. What did her smile look like again? He didn't know which felt worse, the shame of thinking about someone else or the nausea of thinking about Zoe dead. He tried to remind himself that Bianca would probably shoot off both his kneecaps the next time she caught him checking her out, and that idea loosened him up a little. He looked back at Bianca, who was staring straight up, her eyes narrowed in thought.

'So?' Darius said. 'Where do we go now?'

'We look around,' she said, turning and walking down the sidewalk. Darius hurried to catch up.

'There are other skyscrapers, you know. Leon said we need to get to a high point to read this thing—it doesn't have to be the *highest* point.'

'No time,' Bianca muttered, still looking straight ahead.

'How much time do you think we'll waste trying to get up there?'

'Not too much.' Bianca turned to face him and smiled, gesturing to a section of sidewalk completely concealed by tarps. Darius wasn't sure, but he thought he heard the sound of power tools from inside. She started to pull the tarp aside, but Darius stepped past her.

'Let me handle this one,' he said.

'Why?' She squared her shoulders at him and blew a strand of windblown hair out of her face. She would have been almost cute if he didn't know where her weapons were hidden and the way her slender, steel-strong muscles could break bones.

'Because the people in there are underpaid, uninvolved, and don't deserve whatever you're planning to do to them.'

'God! I was just going to knock them out.'

'People die of concussions, you maniac,' Darius replied as he slipped inside the tarp. A man and a woman, both in baggy gray coveralls, looked up as he entered. The man held a large, heavy-looking drill, while the woman had a soldering gun nestled deep in the exposed guts of an elevator control panel.

'Whoa, hey, kid,' the man said, turning off the drill so he could be heard. 'What's the deal?'

'Sorry,' Darius said, holding his hands up with the palms out. He gave them his best self-effacing smile. 'I didn't want to bother you, but my boss sent me.'

'Who's your boss?' the woman said.

'You know the deli about a block from here?' Darius invented.

'Oh, Mel sent you!' the man said, beaming. Darius smiled in relief.

'Yeah,' he said. 'We're doing a lunch special today, limited time. First twenty customers only. Mel told me to come over and let you know. She figured you two would be interested.'

They didn't even wait to hear what the special was. They took off their gloves, stowed their tools, and gave Darius a jarring slap on his shoulder as they hurried past. Bianca slipped in a few seconds later, giving Darius a mischievous half smile.

'Did you have a plan B if that didn't work?' she asked.

'Most of my backup plans lately have amounted to "Bianca beats the crap out of everybody and we run."'

'I'll take that as a compliment,' she said as she bent down

99

and pulled a crowbar from the workers' bags. She jammed it into the freight elevator's doors and pried them open without much apparent effort. A strong, cold wind howled down through the elevator shaft between the cracks of the door, tingling Darius's skin as they entered the elevator.

'Hey,' Darius said as the elevator lurched into motion. 'Is this safe?'

'Relatively speaking, yes.'

The elevator shuddered and ground to a halt for a moment before picking up again.

'Well, that's comforting.'

Bianca, taking advantage of the short period with no witnesses around, took out her pistol and disengaged the safety.

'You expect to use that when we get to the top?'

'Not really, no,' she said. 'But I'd rather have a weapon and nothing to use it on than the other way around.'

'Fair enough.' He let another few seconds of silence pass, rocking back on his heels and patting his hands on his legs. The elevator shuddered again, harder this time, and something above them gave off a worrying metallic groan.

'So, um . . . what do you do for fun?' Bianca said. Darius looked over and saw how wide her eyes had gone. It was the first indication he'd gotten that she even *felt* fear, and it sent an electric wave down his spine. Seeing Bianca rattled was like being a toddler and finding out your parents were scared of the monsters under your bed. 'Besides lying, I mean.'

'Agent Grosz called it *intelligence*.' The elevator started moving again, but much slower this time. 'Film,' he said, finally. 'And photography, I guess.'

'So you like movies? What kind of hobby is that?'

'No, I like to *make* movies, and I like to *watch* films.'

'Oh,' she said. There was a soft tone as the elevator stopped on the first of the levels closed for maintenance. 'Here I thought you would have been a musician. Do you have any of your work back at the base?'

'It's all online,' Darius said, thinking suddenly of how he had just ridden a time machine, killed a man, and fought off a crazed gunwoman on a New York subway, and yet his silly videos were still uploaded on the Internet, and everyone all over the world was still busy with their schools, their jobs, their families. He thought about all the times he'd felt bored and restless, and wondered how strange the world could get without breaking.

'Maybe,' Bianca said, hesitating for a moment as the elevator shook, then resettled, 'maybe when we get back we can watch some of them.'

'That'd be fun.' Darius wondered what Bianca would think of his films, most of them starring Zoe, all shot in the hot, crowded streets of Memphis. 'What about you—what do you do for fun? Besides, you know, beat people up.'

'Ha,' she said sarcastically, rechecking her weapons and avoiding his gaze. 'Not that different from you, actually. Art.'

'You . . . paint? Sketch? Make pottery?'

She laughed, and suddenly Darius's fingers itched for his camcorder, so he could trap this moment in time forever— the way the whole elevator seemed somehow lighter, as though her laughter was lifting it up. 'Art history,' she corrected. 'I don't make the art, just study it. My favorites are American landscapes, from the 1800s. They made the whole world feel so wide, and endless, and . . . *free*, you know?'

'I don't know,' Darius confessed. 'Maybe when we get back you can show me.'

They both turned as the elevator doors opened to reveal a forest of hanging sheets and exposed beams.

'Okay,' Bianca said. 'Let's run the scan and get out of here before someone starts shooting at us.'

'Well, nobody's trying to kill us this very second,' Darius quipped.

The lights went out with a series of loud clicks, leaving them both in complete darkness.

'You were saying?' Bianca hissed.

'Probably just an outage. Exposed wiring or something.' Darius's voice quivered.

Heavy, booted footsteps echoed from farther down the hall.

'Shut up,' Bianca said. 'Stop making it worse. Stand right here and I'll do my best not to kill you too.'

'Wait!' Darius reached out to grab her, but she was already gone. He shuffled blindly forward, mostly out of panic but also, he realized, because he was worried about her. He told himself she would be fine—this was Bianca, after all— but thoughts of her mixed confusingly with his worries over Zoe, churning his stomach in a mix of paralyzing fear.

Suddenly, the hallway was filled with gunfire. He bent over, covering his ears and trying to scream, but each shot still shook him to his core and tore at his eardrums, turning the world into a nightmare of blinding lights and high-pitched whines. Brief flashes of lurid light illuminated the darkness. He could see Bianca in dozens of small snapshots, like a strobe light: jamming a knife into one man's heart while shooting another in the throat, kicking a woman's knee so it bent in the wrong direction, using the same woman as a twitching human shield. His heart pumped frantically, trying to keep up with the flickering nightmares in front of him.

He didn't even register the *ding* from behind him until it was too late, and a gun barrel was pressed into the back of his head.

'I win,' said the woman from the subway. There was another loud series of clicks. Darius flinched, assuming she had pulled the trigger, but instead of a sudden explosion in his head there was a flash of brightness as the lights came back on. The woman cried out in alarm and pulled the gun away from his head.

'DOWN!' he heard Bianca yell, and he dropped to his stomach just as one final gunshot rang through the hallway. A body collapsed behind him with a heavy thud.

Bianca ran over to crouch and put a hand on his shoulder. He tensed and scrabbled away from her, almost getting to his feet but tripping on the subway woman's body. He spared the body a glance, saw what was left of her face, and bit his knuckle, stifling a sob. He thought he might be sick.

'We're safe, Darius,' Bianca said. 'Calm down.'

There was blood splattered all over her—on her arms, chest, and neck, with a few droplets sprayed across her face. But the most surprising thing of all was that she was smiling. Darius took a deep breath, trying to choke back the bile rising in his throat, but it took every ounce of his willpower. Bianca was *smiling*. He swallowed again and tried to look away from her predator's eyes.

'You killed them all,' Darius murmured. He barely heard his own voice over the ringing that still filled his ears.

'Is that an accusation?' she almost yelled. 'They wanted to kill *us*. The woman had a gun to your head! For God's sake, Darius, you killed a man yourself less than an hour ago.'

He nodded. 'You're right,' he managed.

'I know. Now follow me. We've still got work to do.'

'Sure thing. Right behind you.'

They made their way to the stairwell and walked the last three floors up to the observation deck. The place looked like a haunted house, the howling wind from the other side of the canvas-covered windows only adding to the effect. Bianca walked to one of the windows, pulled out the hand-held computer, and started tapping at the screen. She looked for all the world like any sixteen-year-old girl playing with a smartphone, except for the blood-red leopard spots splattered all over her body.

'Okay,' Bianca said. 'Looks like it's in Times Square. Beyond that, I can't get more specifics.'

'Great. So we have to find an object of unknown size and shape in one of the busiest intersections in the world?' Darius asked with a sigh.

'Yep. Just another day at the office.'

Chapter Thirteen

21:00 remaining

Bianca turned left and right, looking over her shoulder at her reflection in the dressing room mirror. Darius had insisted that she get rid of her bloody clothes, and, though she hated the delay, she couldn't deny that walking around covered in gore made her stand out. She'd chosen darker colors this time, black stretchy jeans and a midnight-blue cardigan over a red tank top. She made sure her weapons were hidden under the baggy cardigan and nodded to herself. Leaving her old, bloodstained clothes in a heap on the dressing room floor, she strode quickly to the small boutique's register.

'I'm wearing these out,' Bianca said. She handed the cashier the tags she'd torn off the clothes. The girl looked down at the tags, frowned, and then looked slowly back up. She was silent for a long moment. 'Did I do something wrong?' asked Bianca.

'You know what?' the girl said, scooping up the tags and scanning each one. 'It's fine. They don't pay me enough to care about whatever's happening here. Your total comes to $123.45.'

'What?' Bianca said, slapping her palms down on the counter. The girl flinched and Bianca realized she'd screamed. She coughed and lowered her voice. 'Did you scan something more than once? That's *insane*.'

'Welcome to Manhattan,' the girl said, shrugging. 'Do you want the clothes or not?'

'Fine,' Bianca said. She reached into her messenger bag, pulled out a roll of crisp, freshly printed hundred-dollar bills, and threw two at the cashier. 'Have a nice day!' she said. She ran out before the girl could respond, leaving her staring slack-jawed out at the street.

She walked back to the corner where she'd left Darius, but unsurprisingly, he wasn't there. She sighed in annoyance, swearing under her breath, and looked up and down the block. His Afro peeked out over the crowd across the street.

She stomped over angrily, fuming more and more the closer she got.

He nodded absentmindedly as she approached, not taking his eyes from a building across the street.

'You didn't wait at the corner,' she said.

'Looks like you found me,' he replied. 'It's not like you need to be scared of anything.'

She imagined how she must have looked to him during the fight in the Empire State Building. She remembered the way his hands had shaken, how the blood had drained from his face when he looked at the splatter all over her clothes. Her stomach twisted with shame, and she tried to shove it down. 'Why did you come over here?'

He pursed his lips and looked down, his eyes drifting back to the apartment building across the street. Oh. This was where *she* lived. Bianca's shame quickly turned into disgust. Why should she feel ashamed for doing her job, and doing it well? She was a killer, sure, but he was a liar, and at least she only killed bad men. Worse, he was letting sentimentality get in the way of their job. Any other time, or any other team member, she would have dressed him down; but she was tired, and this felt strangely like new territory. Bianca grabbed his wrist and pulled him back to their original route. He dug his heels in, refusing to move. She turned, ready to explode, but Darius spoke first.

'Bianca?' he said. 'Why do we do this? Go on these missions?'

'To save the world,' she said, swallowing her anger as best she could.

'But why *us*?'

'Because we're the only people in a position to do it. Part of growing up is doing things you don't want to do because they have to be done.'

'But we're not grown up. We're still kids.'

'Speak for yourself. Now can we go?'

He hesitated again, staring at the apartment building, then nodded. 'Have you ever been in love?' he asked quietly.

'Sure,' she said, as she turned and headed back to their original route. 'We all make mistakes.'

When Bianca saw the dazzling lights of Times Square a few blocks later, just as the sun started to sink below the horizon, she literally stopped in her tracks. She had never seen so much *color* in one place. She wondered if Darius, who hadn't spent his entire childhood in an underground world of grays and whites and concrete, wanted to gasp and clap as much as she suddenly did. When she saw the man on the corner wearing nothing but a cowboy hat and a guitar, she burst out laughing.

'It's all just ads, isn't it?' Darius said, looking around.

Bianca spun in a slow circle, ostensibly looking for the rest of the team but also absorbing as much of the kaleidoscope as she could before leaving it behind. Darius was right, of course. The whole thing was an exercise in commercialism, with dozens of pulsing, glittering ads and illuminated storefronts, but she didn't care. She barely even knew what the products on the high-tech screens were. It was all just visual candy to her.

'Do you think they misunderstood our message?' Darius asked, pursing his lips. Bianca had commed Leon soon after they left the Empire State Building.

'Of course we understood,' a voice said behind him. They both spun. Bianca instinctively whipped out her knife, but Malik grabbed her wrist warningly. Leon stifled a laugh while Constance absentmindedly chewed on a Pop-Tart.

'What took you so long?' Bianca demanded, hiding her relief.

'We've been waiting for you!' Constance said, her mouth full. 'But no worries. You gave us time to hit the Pop-Tart store.'

'They have a *whole store*? Just for—never mind,' Bianca said. Constance offered her a silver package and she shook her head. 'Enough sightseeing. This isn't a vacation. It's time to get to work.'

Chapter Fourteen

20:45 remaining

Bianca and Leon were huddled over Leon's handheld computer, speaking in rapid tones about which locations made the most sense as a hiding place for the device. Darius and Constance stood off to the side with Malik, supporting him beneath his shoulders while they watched the crowds pass. Darius had been worried at first that someone might stop and try to help their injured teammate, but everyone just kept moving, avoiding eye contact. He took another bite of Pop-Tart, S'mores flavor, and observed the people. It was the sort of thing he used to do back in Memphis: trying to tell the tourists from the locals, and figuring out how the various groups were related. He wondered what he'd have thought if he had seen Bianca and the others back then. Would he have assumed they were friends? Schoolmates?

'The buildings around here are too crowded,' he heard Bianca say. 'There's no way to keep something as sophisticated as the device we're looking for a secret. It has to be hidden somewhere mobile and inconspicuous. Look for a van, or an abandoned vendor cart or something.'

'No,' Leon argued, shaking his head. 'A reaction like what we saw in those photos requires a titanic amount of power, and unless they have some kind of mobile nuclear reactor, and God help us if they do, this thing has to be hooked up to the grid.'

After a few more minutes of people watching, Darius started noticing features on each passing face that resembled the woman from the train. He shook his head in irritation. This job was literally making him see things. But as his mind wandered, he found that the more he watched people passing by, the less he found himself wondering about who they were and where they came from, and the more he started planning how he would kill them if he had to. He shivered. Bianca was rubbing off on him.

He glanced up at some of the movie billboards and sighed when he read the titles. There was a huge banner featuring a woman with glowing green eyes and red hair, with MORRIGAN printed across the bottom. Last he'd read it was an attempt to revive the *Lord of the Rings* fantasy craze. When had it come out? It must have been in the last few days. Had he only been with Oberon that long? It felt like forever. He rubbed his eyes, trying to will away the fatigue that was creeping up on him.

But then something across the street caught his eye, and he felt suddenly alert. It was a blue gear at the corner of a low-hanging billboard, more of a street-level banner, really. The rest of the image revealed itself as a gap formed in the crush of people. The words EX MACHINA were scrawled across the top of the mechanical tableau. Darius thought of the background in Ludd's video, with its complex backdrop of spinning gears and blinking microchips, and it all fell into place.

'I know where the device is!' he cried out.

'What?' Bianca said, turning from a diagram of the city's electric grid.

'Remember the video from the briefing?'

'No,' Leon said, sarcastically, 'I'd completely forgotten the wannabe supervillain. Your memory is *amazing*.'

'Shut up, Leon,' Bianca said. 'What are you thinking, Darius?'

'Have either of you ever used animation or film tools?'

They both shook their heads.

'Well, then you wouldn't have known to be impressed by that huge graphic behind Ludd. Something that big and complicated takes hours upon hours of work by professional animators and artists.'

'So?' Bianca said. 'The kind of people we get sent after have egos like Mack trucks. That's exactly the kind of thing they would waste money on.'

In answer, Darius just pointed across the street to the banner.

'I still don't—' Bianca began, but Constance interrupted her.

'*Ex Machina*!' she exclaimed. 'I've been waiting for this movie forever. Oh—*oh*.'

The banner was an exact mirror image of the silhouetted gears on Ludd's video, but the mirror flip, and the addition of colors and details, would have made it impossible to notice if they hadn't known to look. Bianca raised an eyebrow at Darius in approval. They turned and ran over to the banner, followed by their companions.

When they reached the billboard, they saw that there was a small gap between two of the spinning cardboard projections which made up its design, directly beneath the *Ex* in the title.

'All right,' Malik said. 'What now?'

Chapter Fifteen

20:20 remaining

The sounds of Times Square faded to a faint hum as Bianca stared furiously at the billboard. The others were talking among themselves, but she barely registered what they were saying. Until she heard Constance suggest that they blow up the wall.

'Too visible,' Bianca protested. 'Blow our cover.'

Leon mused that the gears might be functional, that they might be some part of the device's mechanism.

'They're made of paper,' Bianca said softly, warping one of the cutouts with her fingers.

Darius mentioned that they could wait for one of Ludd's men to come back and force him to let them in at gunpoint.

'Suicidally loyal,' she countered, frowning at the memory of the woman from the train.

Malik started to make a suggestion, but Bianca held up a hand for silence.

'Form a visual perimeter around me,' she said, as she discreetly pulled her knife from its sheath.

'What are you doing?' Darius said.

'I found a seam.' She stood on her toes and poked the tip of her knife into a faint line, bisecting the banner in the space between two gears. It gave immediately, without so much as a tearing sound. Bianca turned to Darius and smiled, feeling a burst of warmth in her chest as her knife slid effortlessly down, parting the material like curtains. The look of confusion he wore made her wish she'd brought a camera. She poked her head through the break in the banner and blinked at the sudden darkness.

'There's a door back here,' she called out to her team-mates. 'The front wall's solid plate glass, so the billboard would've been visible inside.'

'Can you see anything?' Malik asked.

'No.' Bianca slid more of her body through the seam. 'Too dark. Hang on a sec.' She touched the door and pushed gingerly, holding her breath. It moved easily. 'Door's unlocked. I'm going in.'

The door opened onto an echoing space with concrete walls and wooden floors, lit an ethereal blue by the lights filtered through the banner hung over the windows. The mechanical interplay on the banner cast strange, dancing shadows along the walls and floor, leaving Bianca feeling as though she'd slipped into a dream. She blinked once in confusion; then her training kicked in, and she spun around to check for immediate threats and for exits. The one exit was a steep set of stairs leading up to darkness on the opposite wall from the door. The only other thing in the room was a glossy, waist-high black cube small enough to fit in the trunk of a car, sitting squarely in the middle of the floor. A green number pad lit up the side facing them, with a red bar at the top. Bianca assumed the numbers were some kind of countdown readout.

'Come in. Hurry!' she called out, but the others were already making their way inside. They deposited Malik carefully against the glass wall. Leon and Constance drifted over to the device, while Darius stayed by the door, keeping the street outside in his peripheral vision.

'We still have a lot of time,' Bianca said. She walked over and leaned down to more closely inspect the readout. 'Think this is the timer? It looks like it's getting smaller, like kind of a reverse loading bar.'

She always felt oddly relaxed at moments like these. They'd found the threat—and more importantly, removed the danger of the twenty-four-hour time limit. Now all they had to do was complete the mission and get home. This, Bianca could handle. It was the thought of disappearing into a dead time line, like Isaac had, that still gave her nightmares.

'Kind of ruins the dramatic tension,' Darius said.

'Some of us have had enough drama for one day, thank you very much,' Malik interrupted. He winced at an unfortunate bend of his injured leg.

Leon joined Bianca beside the device and kneeled, unrolling what looked like a blue sheet of cellophane stretched between two rods. He flattened the sheet against one side of the device and pressed a button on the top rod. The material buzzed and glowed as it revealed an interior view of the device. Leon examined the innards for a moment, moving his makeshift window to different sides for a better view. He snorted after a moment and rolled the film back up, stowing it in his backpack.

'Hey, Connie,' he said. 'Did you bring your plasma torch?'

Bianca stepped aside to give Constance room as she walked over, slinging her tool bag off her shoulder.

'You're just going to burn your way into it?' Bianca said, appalled at her usually meticulous teammate's sudden casual streak. Was Darius rubbing off on everyone? Constance slipped on a pair of opaque goggles and gestured for all of them to look away as she started up the blinding light on her torch. Bianca covered her eyes and listened to the caustic hiss as the tool's flame ate away at the device's outer casing.

'It's just molded plastic with metal bracings holding up the detonator,' Leon explained. 'Except I guess it isn't an explosive, so *detonator* isn't the right word. They're holding up the . . .' He tapped his chin and squinted in thought.

'Thingy,' Constance provided, without looking up.

'Whatever,' Bianca said. 'Aren't there security measures, though? Couldn't you accidentally set it off?'

'I doubt it.' Leon shrugged. 'As far as I can tell it's just a gimmicky piece of tech slapped inside a pretty, futuristic-looking shell.'

He leaned down and peeked into the hole Constance had burned into the device.

'Quiet, everyone,' Darius hissed suddenly. He leaned to the side, getting a better look at the street. Leon and Constance froze in the middle of handing tools to each other.

'What is it?' Bianca grabbed for her knife.

'There's a cop coming close.'

'Has he seen us?' Leon said.

'It doesn't look like it.'

'Then shut up.' Leon rolled his eyes as he returned to work.

Bianca relaxed the grip on her knife and let out a long

breath, trying not to laugh at the way Darius pursed his lips. Her smile evaporated when he turned to face her, looked over her shoulder, and gasped in alarm. Bianca didn't wait for him to call out. She spun in place and threw her knife in one smooth motion. There was a brief glimpse of white-and-black armor before the knife hit home, bouncing off the Luddite's rifle with a shower of sparks. Bianca bolted up the stairs, lunging in to strike the man before he could realign his aim.

He pivoted out of the way, a muffled grunt audible through his helmet as he drove the butt of his rifle into Bianca's shoulder. She gasped and curled into a ball, forcing herself to stay conscious. The man raised his rifle again, preparing to bring it down on Bianca's skull. She glanced down the stairs and saw Malik propped up against the far wall, sweating in pain, aiming his sidearm at the Luddite. She scissored her legs across the Luddite's knees and he fell, his rifle clipping Bianca on the temple as he tumbled down the stairs.

Bianca stood up, her vision swimming. Her right eye stung, and the world turned red. She wiped at her forehead, feeling blood on her fingers. She could feel her heartbeat behind her eyes, and the way the stairs seemed to tilt back and forth only made her head hurt more. Constance had picked up the Luddite's rifle from where it fell. The man himself was back on his feet, a long combat knife in hand.

Leon stood between him and Malik, his own pistol raised but shaking. Darius had left the room sometime in the last few seconds, but there was no time to wonder what had happened to him. Bianca picked up her own knife from the stair above her and lurched down the stairs. She leaped toward the man once her feet hit the floor. He turned at the last minute and put one of his arms between his throat and Bianca's knife. The blade slid between the bones of his forearm, staining his white armor a vibrant red. He screamed, but the helmet cut most of the volume. He kneed Bianca in the stomach and they both fell to the floor, Bianca coughing and retching.

'Is there a problem, officer?' Darius's voice cut through the banging and scraping. Bianca pinned the man's knife hand to the ground and took a quick look around the room. Constance motioned toward the door and raised a finger to her lips. The man heaved forward. Bianca twisted her knife, grinding it against the man's arm bones. He groaned and shuddered but still managed to climb on top of her. He tore his knife hand out of her grip and poised it above her neck.

'Can you tell me what you're doing here, son?' an older male voice said.

'Just some filming,' Darius said. 'Me and my friends are doing a documentary for our film class.'

Bianca jerked her upper body to the side as the knife

fell. It stuck in the wood of the floor with a soft *thunk*. The man gave a muffled curse and pulled his arm off Bianca's knife, trying to get to his feet. Bianca struggled to follow him, but another wave of dizziness sent her stumbling back into a crouch. The man kicked her in the side, knocking her breath out.

'Did you and your friends cut that billboard open?' the officer said.

'Nah,' Darius said. 'It was taped together. Seems like it'd be a pretty huge violation of the fire code if they sealed up a door like that, wouldn't it?'

The man fumbled at a pistol hooked onto his belt, but Constance leaped forward and swung the rifle at his head like a club. He fell and groaned, opening and closing his hands as he tried to push himself up to his hands and knees. Bianca hissed, coughed a few painful breaths, and snatched the knife out of the floor as she scrambled over to the fallen man.

'What was that sound?' the police officer said.

Bianca nodded quickly to Constance, who bit her knuckle as she hurried around to sit on the man's knees. Bianca pushed on his chest with one knee and dug her heel into his uninjured palm, crouching so their faces almost touched.

'Our sound guy is working on the special effects. Don't they sound good? The acoustics in there are pretty sweet.'

'Mm-hmm,' the officer said. 'Son, I'm going to need you to step aside.'

'Come on, sir! The light's fading, and this is our last day to shoot.'

The man pulled at his gun with his bleeding arm. He managed to get it off his belt, but his hand was shaking so violently that he could barely lift it, let alone point it at Bianca. She snatched it from him, ejected the clip, and tossed the gun itself to Constance. Then she leaned over and whispered into the soldier's helmet, trying to avoid her reflection in his dark goggles.

'Would you walk away, if I gave you the offer?'

Leon caught her gaze. He looked furious as he mouthed, *What!?* Bianca scowled at him and turned back to the prisoner.

'I said to step aside,' the cop said outside. 'This is your last warning.'

Bianca could hear the man's breathing. Even through the hardened plastic of his helmet. It was ragged and panicked.

'You really want me to show your supervisors this video, Officer . . . Dunn? The cameras are rolling,' Darius said, his tone shifting from friendly to flat.

'Are you threatening me, kid?' the officer said.

'I asked you a question,' Bianca whispered again. 'Nod or shake your head, please.' The ringing returned to her ears. The man nodded slowly.

'I'm just saying, the NYPD might find it interesting to know that you spent the last half hour smoking, and that instead of looking for the real criminals who are probably lurking around Times Square, you're harassing a bunch of teenagers.'

Bianca held her breath. The entire room went silent, except for a soft whimper of pain from the man beneath her.

'I'm coming back in thirty minutes,' Officer Dunn said. 'I don't care what you've seen; I want you gone by then. Got it?'

'Absolutely,' Darius said, suddenly all warmth again. He squeezed back through the seam and yelled, 'Have a nice day, sir!' He turned and froze once he'd entered the room, taking in the scene with wide eyes.

'Good job,' Malik said.

'You can lose the puppy face,' Bianca said. 'He's alive. And he wants to stay alive for a long time. Don't you?'

The man nodded again, slowly.

'I'm going to get up now,' Bianca said. 'I want you to stay completely still. I get a little edgy when people try to break my ribs.'

Constance got up and walked over to Darius while Bianca moved carefully to a crouch by the man's uninjured arm. Her breathing was coming back to normal, and her balance was returning. She let her hands hang between her knees and waited a moment before speaking again.

'You're going to tell us everything you know about Ludd,' she said.

'No,' the man said. 'I won't.' His helmet made him sound like he was speaking from the other room, but Bianca still picked up a chord of sadness in his voice. His uninjured hand snapped up to his neck before Bianca could move. There was a click and a tiny hydraulic hiss. The next few seconds were filled with screams, then whimpers, and then gurgles as the man thrashed on the floor, his back and limbs twisting in unnatural, frantic motions. He was quiet again by the time Leon reached him and removed his helmet.

Bianca clenched her teeth. He was . . . had been beautiful, and like the woman from the train, in his early twenties. He had dirty blond hair, matted with sweat, and bright blue eyes which now matched the light blue tint to his skin. Bianca ran a hand down her face and turned away, trying not to look Darius in the face.

'It's okay,' Darius said. 'You tried.'

'*Trying* doesn't cut it,' Bianca said. 'I should have seen that coming.'

'Yeah, yeah,' Leon said. Bianca turned to see him leaning against the device, a smug expression on his face. 'It's really depressing that the psycho killed himself so he wouldn't have to help us save millions of lives. On the other hand, your *amazing* friend Leon just disabled this piece of junk.'

Chapter Sixteen

20:12 remaining

Leon returned to work immediately, mumbling something about wanting to get to know his new girlfriend better. Constance made a nauseated face, and Bianca just shook her head. Darius wondered if Leon was really that oblivious or if his was a calculated persona meant to keep people at bay. If that was the case, he was doing such a good job not even Darius could see through it.

Darius started to say something but then he noticed Malik making a lewd gesture at Leon's back. Constance blushed and mouthed, *That's mean!* while Darius held back a laugh. He thought he saw Bianca crack a smile.

'So,' he said. 'Where do we go from here?'

'Workshop,' Constance said, her tongue poking out the side of her mouth as she went back to tinkering with part of the device's guts.

'Infirmary,' Malik said.

'Mess hall,' Bianca said.

'Back home?' Darius asked, then realized his choice of words. When had Oberon become home? He realized he felt genuinely relieved at the idea of returning, although considering where he was returning *from*, it probably wasn't surprising. 'We're not going after Ludd?'

'Not part of the mission,' Malik said. 'Our job is to negate a suitably catastrophic event and get home before the clock runs out. Everything else is handled in real time by the actual military. *Maybe* an intelligence agency, if the incident is small enough.'

'Besides,' Bianca said, 'we don't even know where to find him.'

'About that,' Leon said. He removed a pair of opaque goggles with shaking hands and stood up, frowning. 'This device was a decoy.'

'That's not funny!' Constance cried out. Leon fixed her with a distant, haunted expression. He always seemed a little morbid and sleep-deprived, but now he looked like he'd seen his own death. Darius wondered if he'd looked like that when Grosz showed him the picture in the diner, back in Memphis.

'What do you mean, Leon?' Malik asked, speaking in soft, even tones, like a negotiator trying to contain a hostage situation.

'There are more of them,' Leon said. 'I found the rest of the codes I needed to break into Ludd's comm network inside that thing. The devices are monitored remotely, so I figured they all relayed to the same location. Once I found that, the rest was easy to trace.'

The background noises of honking horns and hundreds of bustling people flowed into the silence of the room. Constance's eyes had gone wide and glassy, like a skittish animal caught in headlights. Malik groaned and thumped the back of his head against the wall. Bianca wrapped her arms around her stomach, glancing at the body on the floor so quickly that Darius imagined he was the only one to notice. She looked back up at him, and she seemed, suddenly, very old.

'How many more?' she asked quietly.

'Three.'

A ball of ice formed in Darius's stomach. He ran his hands over his hair and slid down to sit with his back against the wall.

'From what I can tell,' Leon said, 'they're set to go off in a little over—'

'Twenty-two hours,' Darius cut in. 'Or somewhere between twenty-one and twenty-two, I'm not sure.'

'Yeah,' Leon said, giving Darius a suspicious look.

'We should have known, then!' Constance exclaimed, her voice pitching up. 'That was right when we left!'

'No.' Darius sighed. 'It was probably a few minutes after we left. Or will be a few minutes after. Not sure what tense to use, but still.' He drummed his fingers on the floor for a few quiet seconds and thought. Everyone was looking at him now. He did his best to ignore them. 'Is it possible to travel back to the same time twice? Like, if we go back to headquarters now, could we then come back twenty-four hours again?'

'Nobody really knows,' Malik said. 'It's the commander's position that nothing is worth the risk of . . . what was it?'

'A tachyon cascade,' Leon said. 'The engineers believe there's a risk of a tachyon cascade if you create and then snip off too many time lines. And before you ask, it means the dissolution of space-time. So no, there are no second tries.'

'Then he knew we were coming,' Darius said. The others looked at him strangely. He almost wanted to laugh. How was he the only one to see it? Did they all believe in Oberon too firmly? 'I had a feeling—he knew everything, where the door was and which routes we would take. But I wasn't sure, until now. This leaves no room for doubt.'

'But how did he even know we *exist*?' Bianca breathed. 'Oberon is one of the most secret organizations on the planet. The only people outside Oberon who know about it get their lives rewritten if they try to tell a single person about us.'

'Then it must not have been someone outside the organization,' Malik said slowly.

Darius gave him a mirthless smile. 'However he did it, it's done now. No one can stop the other three bombs.'

'Except us,' Constance said.

'How? Where are the other devices?' Darius asked.

'Tokyo, London, and San Francisco,' Leon said.

'See? He has to have known we couldn't reach all three cities in less than twenty-one hours.'

'Actually, we can.' Bianca was chewing her lip and staring off into the middle distance. 'But it doesn't matter.' She cut the air with her hand to signal the conversation's end. 'We're done. Pack up. We're heading home.'

'Wait,' Darius said. 'We *can*? And yet you're just going to let all those people die?'

'You want to stay?' Bianca snapped. The others stayed silent, looking down at their feet.

'Not really, no. But isn't it our responsibility?'

Bianca spun to face him with a wide-eyed, frantic expression that scared Darius more than anything he'd seen from her yet. 'You want to die? Because if you're right, then he left just enough men in New York to challenge us without raising any suspicion. And look at Malik! And you—you would have died without me! There could be hundreds more out there, better armed and better trained. You'll die slowly from a bullet in the stomach and never see the girl in that building again. Or maybe we disarm the devices! It's possible. We *might* be able to make it to all three locations in eighteen hours, but only barely. A best-case scenario leaves us with maybe an hour and a half to spare before we need to reach a gate.'

'But *millions* of people—'

'Are *irrelevant!*' she said, her voice quavering. 'We came here in a *machine that unravels the fabric of the universe!* You don't improvise with the kind of forces we deal with, you *child*. There are protocols. There's a plan. There's a mission. We stick to them, and when they work and we save lives, that's great. But when you deviate from the mission, no matter what your intentions, the worst-case scenario is always worse than you can imagine.'

'I can't imagine a worse outcome than what will happen if we give up now,' Darius said. 'Maybe I'm naive. It doesn't change what's right and wrong, though.'

Darius ground his teeth and tried to calm his breathing. He felt nauseous. Why, exactly, was he doing this? He thought of the bed waiting for him back in his dorm, and all the meals he didn't need to steal, and how nobody would shoot at him, and how he wouldn't be erased from existence.

He thought of the woman from the train, and how her mother would feel if she could see her daughter's beautiful face, cold in death. He looked at the dead young man next to the device.

Then he thought of Zoe. He wondered what she was doing right now—reading, probably. She wouldn't have finished unpacking yet, even after a few days. She would be sitting on the floor, cross-legged, leaning against a stack of cardboard boxes, unaware of how close she had come to hell. The image made his chest feel warm, but the feeling was quickly evaporated by a wave of guilt as he pictured all the other Zoes, all the other sons, sisters, mothers, and friends, in the millions, who would die if he did what the coward in his head wanted him to.

'We have to try,' he said.

'Weren't you listening?' Bianca's voice was shaking.

'Yeah. And I'm sorry you lost someone close to you, but that just means you should know better than anyone the value of saving even one life. You can't bring Isaac back, but you can stop millions of people from feeling the way you do.'

A smear of glowing red spread across Bianca's cheeks and nose, and she stormed out. Darius started to follow, but Malik put a hand on his shoulder.

'Give her a minute,' he said.

'Why? Will she beat me up again?'

'That's not fair,' Constance said. 'She has a lot of responsibilities, and she works harder than any of us. I don't think she would recover if she knew we'd seen her cry.'

'Cry?' Darius said. He had assumed the red in her face was rage. He tried to imagine Bianca hugging herself and sobbing, but couldn't quite put the picture together. Bianca came back inside after a moment of awkward silence. Her face was dry, but the skin around her eyes was puffy and the eyes themselves were glossy and pink.

'Why are you all standing around?' she said. 'We've got a plane to catch.'

Chapter Seventeen

19:40 remaining

The crowds were just as dense on Forty-Ninth Street as they had been in Times Square, and just as ambivalent. Nobody seemed to bat an eye at the pair of grubby-looking teenagers with a drill and a flat head screwdriver working on a hot rod worth more than their educations. Granted, Bianca wasn't that experienced with the way things worked outside Oberon, but she had a hard time imagining what people thought was going on. Darius seemed to know what he was doing, though, so she closed her eyes and leaned against the hood, trying not to think about anything.

Darius had insisted they put some distance between themselves and Times Square before they found transportation, and Bianca hadn't argued. That police officer probably wasn't joking about coming back in half an hour, and after all the violence of the day, she didn't want to have to knock out a cop. The others had drifted over to an ice-cream shop across the street, but Darius had asked Bianca to stay with him, insisting that he needed her help, though she wasn't sure what she could do.

There was a plastic *clunk* from inside the car. Darius leaned out and waved at Bianca. 'Could I get a hand?' he said. She shrugged and walked over. He gave her the screwdriver and picked up the drill.

'What do I do with this?' Bianca said.

'Hold it.' He fired up the drill, pressed it against the keyhole, and started drilling, the metallic whine making conversation impossible for a moment. A few people turned at the sound of the drill, but they only spared it a glance before moving on their way.

'I wanted to say—' he started, but Bianca sensed an earnest, serious conversation looming, so she cut in.

'Why this car?' she asked.

'I don't rob poor people,' Darius replied as he got out of the driver's seat. 'But most expensive cars nowadays have either a keyless entry or a computer in the engine, and both make hot-wiring a mess.'

'Oh,' Bianca said. 'And this is an expensive car from before those features existed?'

'Yeah,' Darius said. He gave her a half smile and turned to watch the others approach. 'That, and I wanted to do something nice for Constance.'

Bianca started to ask him what he meant, but she was interrupted by Constance yelling, 'No way!' as she and the rest of the team walked back across the street. She ran toward them, an ice-cream cone in each hand, and bent over next to the car. Darius slapped a hand on her back, drawing her out of her gearhead hypnosis.

'Come on,' he said. 'You're getting ice cream everywhere. There'll be time to drool once we're on the road.'

'Right,' she said, but the smile stayed plastered on her face. She turned and handed Bianca a two-scoop monstrosity of light and dark brown.

'It's chocolate-chip cookie dough and fudge and chocolate cheesecake,' she said. 'You seemed like you needed it.'

Bianca and Constance didn't have much in common, and Bianca resented the feeling she got from the others that they should be friends just because they were both girls. But every now and then there was a twinkle of understanding in Constance that made Bianca glad she was on the team. She hugged Constance and thanked her. She gave Leon a look which dared him to say something, but he was too engrossed in his handheld computer to care anyway.

The sedan's engine purred to life, and Darius got out, gesturing to Constance with a flourish and a cocksure smile.

'You *can* drive stick, can't you?' Darius asked.

'Do red shirts die on *Star Trek*?' Constance said through a mouthful of ice cream.

Darius blinked slowly and said, 'Uh . . . yes?' Constance ran around and jumped in the driver's seat.

'I'll need you to hold this for me, though,' she said, handing Darius her cone. He moved to the passenger seat. Bianca and Leon helped Malik into the back and then piled in themselves.

'You can have some if you want,' Constance told Darius as they pulled out into traffic. 'I wish you would have let me get you one. It's not like it's even my money.'

'No, it's fine,' Darius said. He sounded far off, like he was thinking about something. He turned in his seat to better face Bianca and the rest in the back. 'You're sure this is okay?'

'Don't act like this is the first car you've stolen,' Bianca said.

'It is, actually.'

'You did a pretty good job for a beginner.'

'You pick stuff up,' he said with a grin. 'I needed some money. I asked a friend to show me how. I chickened out at the last minute.'

'Didn't want to do time?'

Darius nodded. 'For all the difference it's made.'

'Well, don't worry,' Bianca said. 'We'll leave the car at JFK with a note on the hood that says it's stolen.'

'Why JFK?'

'Oberon's secret airfield,' Leon said.

'How can it be a secret?' Darius said. 'Isn't JFK one of the busiest airports in the country?'

'I don't know,' Bianca said. 'I don't really travel a lot. But it's better to have it here than out in the middle of nowhere.'

'How do you figure?'

'You of all people should know that the best place to hide something is where no one would think to look for it,' Malik said. 'Even if that means sitting right out in the open.'

Darius nodded slowly. 'So you're telling me Oberon has planes that can go around the world in less than twenty-four hours.'

'We're not the only ones who have access to them,' Constance explained.

'And the government just leaves them in the busiest airports on the planet.'

'The doors *are* locked,' Leon said.

When they pulled up to JFK—through a back entrance that Darius would never have known was there if Constance hadn't pointed it out—a bearded man in aviator sunglasses and dirty blue coveralls was sitting in front of a barb-wire gate in a folded lawn chair. He looked up from a magazine and nodded at Bianca as she approached.

'I need a ride,' she said.

'What's your name?' He scratched at his beard.

'My dad's friends call him Puck.'

The man tossed his magazine aside, stood up, and entered a code into the keypad beside the hangar doors. They opened, revealing two old-looking but still impressive private jets. 'Come on in,' he said. 'We'll discuss your charter in more detail inside.'

Bianca got out of the car, and the rest of the team followed suit. The place smelled like dust and jet fuel. Some power tool Constance probably could have identified whined behind the farthest jet.

'These can't be our rides,' Darius said. 'These look . . . *normal*.'

'It's what's on the inside that counts, kid,' the bearded man said. He patted the nose of the nearest plane and smiled. 'Now who wants to tell me where we're headed?'

'I've got it,' Leon said. He and the bearded man walked over to a second pilot, getting his attention over the sound of his work.

Malik gave Bianca a short nod toward the far wall, indicating that he wanted to talk. Bianca nodded back. 'Me and Mal are going to go talk plans. Constance, I need you and Darius to check our gear and load the planes.'

'Got it.'

'Good.' Bianca helped Malik over to the far wall and sat him down on the floor. He immediately unrolled a thin blanket and started disassembling his rifle.

'I have some things to say. I've kept silent until now because I respect authority and I didn't want to call you out in front of the group.' He kept his eyes locked on his work as he methodically oiled and wiped down every moving part in his weapon.

'Okay.' Bianca smoothed her hair behind her ears and joined him, pressing her back into the cold wall of the hangar. She knew better than to offer a helping hand in his maintenance. Malik was usually the calmest person she knew, but after all their time together, she knew how to recognize the signs that a storm was brewing under his exterior. 'What's up?'

'You know the protocol.'

'I do,' Bianca said. 'I had it memorized before any of you were recruited.'

'None of our missions have ever had a scope like this.'

'I know,' Bianca said. She felt her fists clench without any input from her brain. Her nails dug into her palms.

'Do you know why you're our leader?'

'Because I have the most experience.'

'You were more experienced than Isaac, but *he* was our leader.' He locked the barrel back onto the stock with a loud click.

'How *dare*—' Bianca began, feeling the blood rise to her face.

'No, how dare *you*,' Malik interrupted, slamming into her with a flick of his dark-rimmed eyes. 'I have been patient with you, because you were not taken from a full, promising life like the rest of us. You were a small child. Your future *changed*, while the rest of us lost ours.'

'You have no idea what I've been through!' Bianca hissed.

'I know that we have all been through a lot, and the rest of us find ways to deal with it that won't get everyone close to us killed.'

Bianca ran a hand across her face and sighed. She saw Darius at the other end of the hangar, tugging on a satchel he could barely lift. 'It doesn't change that he's right. We have a moral responsibility.'

'We have a personal responsibility not to get ourselves killed over an impossible task. And last time I checked you two were at each other's throats, then he drops Isaac's name while he browbeats you about morality, and you actually listen to him. You would have attacked any one of us for saying the same.'

'Maybe I'm tired of being the hard one all the time,' she said, remembering the horrified look Darius had given her every time she'd killed.

'Well,' Malik said as he rolled up his tools and placed his gun across his lap, 'I thought your little feud was kind of cute at first, and then it got annoying, and now it's probably going to put us all in the ground—*if* it doesn't wipe us out of existence.'

'I take it you're not coming to London with me,' Bianca said.

'You've made the plans already, then?'

'Me and Leon in London,' Bianca said flatly. 'I couldn't deny Constance the chance to visit Tokyo. It was really just a question of where you were going.'

'Don't worry.' Malik winced as he stood up. Bianca offered him a hand, and he gently blocked it, insisting on moving around under his own power. 'I wouldn't have been much help.'

Chapter Eighteen

14:40 remaining

Darius was still groggy from the short nap he'd taken on the flight, and Tokyo's Shibuya Crossing's unending stream of pulsing colors and clashing digital sounds was quickly giving him a headache. It didn't help that Malik, nestled high above Tokyo, had only been able to narrow their search down to nearly six square miles. It would have been close to impossible to find the Times Square device without the billboard clue. Darius didn't want to think about the odds on this search. He followed Constance through tides of pedestrians and kept his eyes open, trying to locate what felt like a needle in a haystack.

The radio crackled to life in Darius's ear. 'Any luck?' Malik said, the wind from his high perch making him sound far away—which, Darius thought, he technically was. He seemed tense and bored in his capacity as their support staff; but Darius would have traded the loud, dangerous street for the peaceful view at the top of the Tokyo Skytree in a second, even if it meant a bullet in the leg.

'Constance is having a good time,' Darius said, shaking his head as she snapped a picture of a street performer with antigravity hair dressed in a combination of a sailor suit and cyborg armor. 'No sign of the device or of Ludd's people, though. Not that I would notice them dancing around a foot in front of my face.'

'Are you seeing a bunch of people in weird costumes?'

'How'd you know?'

'I did some searching and it turns out there's an *otaku* convention near there.'

Constance got Darius's attention, pointed to what looked like a nearby candy shop, and mouthed, *Five minutes.* Darius shrugged and returned his attention to Malik.

'"*Otaku*"?' Darius said.

'It's like a Japanese word for nerd. *Otaku* culture revolves around Japanese cartoons, comics, and video games. Costumes are a big part of these conventions, and since a lot of Japanese pop culture involves robots and science fiction . . .'

'They could be anywhere,' Darius said, giving the area another visual sweep. He stopped on half a dozen men and women in formfitting body armor with visored helmets, but none of them had the black-and-white color scheme of the Luddites' armor. What worried Darius was that nobody batted an eye at those in costume, many of whom carried what looked like weapons. Ludd might not even need to *hide* the device here.

A glimpse of white and black drew Darius's eye. If the trundling, eight-foot figure coming around the corner was just a costume, it was the most impressive he had ever seen outside of a multimillion-dollar film. It had huge, armored limbs bristling with gun barrels, missile chambers, and glowing protrusions Darius couldn't begin to name. A crowd surrounded the figure, taking pictures with their phones. The flashes and the press of bodies made it difficult to pick out much color, but Darius was sure the thing was adorned with the same black-and-white pattern as the Luddites from New York. It was headed toward the candy shop Constance had entered. Did they know she was in there? Did they know he was watching them? He ran across the street, figuring that they would have shot him already if they knew who he was. He stormed into the candy shop and stopped beside Constance, panting.

'What's the matter?' Contance said. 'You look like you've seen a— Ooh! Pocky!'

'Constance, you didn't see that thing?'

'Shee whut?' she said through a mouth full of Pocky sticks.

'*Are!*' a woman said, springing up from behind the counter. She waved a hand at Constance, who coughed and did her best to act casual with a face covered in powdered sugar. The woman rounded the counter and walked over to them, gesturing for them to leave as soon as they could. '*Gaijin achi itte!*'

She started pushing them toward the door, but Darius held his hands up, trying to signal that he was sorry but they needed to stay. He held her off long enough for the crowd to pass, the large machine literally shaking the merchandise on the shelves. From up close, Darius could tell it was some kind of man-shaped tank—and his heart sank when he saw what looked like five regular, armored Luddites moving with the crowd. Constance exchanged a glance with him. She took out a wallet, threw a handful of American money at the shopkeeper, and together they rushed back out to the street.

'This is insane,' Constance said. 'Why are they out in the open like this? Where are the police?'

'It's the octopus convention,' Darius said. 'What's the difference between these guys and all the other costumed weirdos?'

'It's *otaku*,' Constance said. She bit her lip. 'They wouldn't be here if the device wasn't also nearby, would they?'

'Probably not,' Darius said. He shrugged. Neither the man in the armored suit nor his five companions had seemed to notice them so far, which allowed him to relax a little. 'Or they're here because they think it's where we'll be.'

'Malik,' Constance said, tapping her earpiece. 'Can you take a look at the scanner for me?'

'Sure,' he said. 'I can't really tell you anything new. It's still somewhere in Shibuya Crossing.'

'You're sure?' Constance said. 'Nothing has changed?'

'No,' Malik said slowly. 'Wait, yes. There's an . . . I don't know. Hold on, I need to go through the notes Leon gave me.'

'Could you hurry?' Constance said.

Darius nodded to Constance and then to the retreating group. She bit her lip and nodded back, following him as he walked after the white-and-black armored hulk, doing his best to seem casual despite the terror clawing at the inside of his chest.

'I'll try,' Malik said. 'I mean, his notes are beyond cryptic, but I'm going as fast as I can.'

'Ask yourself this,' Darius said. '"How fast would I work if my teammates were in spitting distance of a giant suit of mechanical armor covered in guns?"'

'That's not a hypothetical, I take it?' Malik said.

The armored Luddite turned, the sidewalk shaking under its feet. Darius grabbed Constance by the elbow, pulling her behind a parked van. A few seconds passed without the van ripping apart in a tidal wave of fire and lead, so Darius figured they probably hadn't been seen. He let out a long, slow breath.

'Sadly, no,' he said.

'Hold on just a sec,' Malik said. 'Something just changed.'

'What was it?' Constance said, crouching and holding her hand to her earpiece.

Darius stepped away from the van, keeping the armored Luddite in his peripheral vision. The thing was standing still, except for a single, glowing red 'eye' in the center of its eight-foot-high head. The eye moved steadily back and forth, looking for something.

'Well, there's a wavelength monitor on the bottom here,' Malik said, his side of the conversation clear in Darius's earpiece. 'Until just a second ago, every other wave was a lot thinner than the others, but they evened out a few seconds ago. Has anything changed?'

'Not sure,' Constance said. She leaned out from the van and caught his eye. 'Darius?'

He did have one idea, but it was too depressing to think about.

'The compression could have been a result of the device moving relative to the scanner's position,' Constance said.

Oh, no, Darius thought. *Please let me be wrong.*

'Darius, how big is the armor you were talking about?' Malik asked.

Darius groaned and squeezed his eyes shut. 'Big enough to hold a device inside.' His heart started to race uncontrollably. 'Listen, we need to retreat. We need to get in contact with the others somehow. We can't diffuse a bomb when it's inside a tank!'

Constance planted her hands on his shoulders and stared him down. He realized he was hyperventilating and forced himself to take deep, slow breaths.

'Listen to me,' she said. 'Listen to my voice.'

'Y-yeah?' he gasped.

'I have personally sunk an aircraft carrier and a nuclear submarine. One time I blew up a half-dozen rebuilt panzer tanks with nothing but a one-pound block of plastique and a remote-control car. It's my job to find big, mechanical weapons and blow them up.'

'But this is a robot, Constance! Did you know gigantic battle robots even existed, let alone a way to take them out?'

'No,' Constance said. 'But trust me, I can handle this.'

Darius felt his anxiety melt away, replaced by an overwhelming need to laugh. 'You know you're almost as much of a dork as Leon, right?' he said.

'Please,' Constance said, letting him go. 'He doesn't hold

a candle to me. Now, you're our resident trickster. Any ideas?'

Darius peeked back around the van to make sure the armored Luddite was still in place. The crowd had begun dispersing, leaving the lighter Luddites and their armored companion out in the open. They seemed to be talking among themselves.

'I can't think of anything specific,' Darius said. He looked back over his shoulder at Constance. 'I was thinking maybe I could distract them while you come around from the side and . . .'

'And what?' Constance said.

'. . . hack it?'

'Wow,' she said. 'The things you don't know about computers could fill my—' She stopped and looked over his shoulder, the look of terror returning to her face.

'Status report,' Malik said. 'Everybody still in one piece?'

Darius returned his gaze to the sidewalk just in time to see the five Luddites unslinging their rifles from their shoulders. The red eye on the armor's head was focused directly at him. A mechanical whine could be heard coming from somewhere, rapidly increasing in pitch. Darius had a sinking feeling the sound meant one of its weapons was powering up.

'Not for long!' He dove back behind the van and rolled to his feet, taking off after Constance, who was already making a beeline for a nearby alley. There was an ear-splitting wall of sound behind him from five assault rifles and God knew what else firing all at once, followed by a shock wave that nearly sent him head first onto the concrete. He had to jump over a few fallen bystanders, their cries of pain and confusion following him as he stumbled into the alley. Constance stopped near a dumpster and turned.

'Duck!' she screamed. Darius followed her as she huddled behind the dumpster and another barrage of gunfire ripped the air apart.

The high-pitched whine filled the silence again, and a moment later, something flashed so bright and hot that Darius saw red even through his eyelids. He heard Constance screaming next to him, and dimly registered the smell of burned hair. When he finally opened his eyes, he realized the top of the dumpster had been partially melted, partially blasted away, and the rest of the alley was crumbling and charred. The concrete shook, accentuating the thunder of Darius's heartbeat.

'We have to run!' He reached to pull Constance to her feet, but she was still rubbing her eyes.

'I'm blind!' she screamed. She tried to follow him but tripped over a piece of wreckage. She clutched at her bleeding leg and hissed in pain.

'Come on,' Darius said. He could just see the top of the titanic armored Luddite coming toward them, halfway across the street now. He grabbed Constance by the elbow and pulled her back up. 'Come *on*!' The alley ended in a maintenance door, probably locked, but there was a fire escape above them, its bottom ladder already deployed. The bottom rungs were warped from whatever fiery blast had destroyed the dumpster, but Darius was pretty sure he could still reach them. The main flaw with his plan, however, was that the five armed men and their walking tank would rip his body into a puddle of gore the moment he came into view.

'Constance,' Darius said, holding her still to keep her from tripping again. 'We need a distraction. *Please* tell me you have an idea.'

She unslung her bag and pushed it into his arms. 'Front right pocket,' she said. 'Stun grenades.'

'Your right or my right?'

'My right! Also check for a metal disk, about the size of a Frisbee. It's got a button on the side.'

Darius held the small, cylindrical stun grenade in the crook of his elbow and quickly found the second item. 'The button activates it?'

'Just press the button, pull the pin, throw both, and duck. And cover your ears,' Constance said.

Darius did as he was told. The grenade made a small *tink* as the pin escaped, while the disk started frantically blinking. One of the unarmored Luddites cried out in alarm as the grenade landed, and the drumming of the armored Luddites' footsteps ceased. There was another bright pulse of light, accompanied by a wall of sound that would have deafened Darius if he hadn't been warned. Constance tapped his elbow, indicating that it was safe to stand again.

'We have to move fast,' she said. She blinked and shook her head, her eyes watering.

'Can you see well enough to climb?' Darius said.

'I can't see at all.' She gave the wall an impatient frown that was probably meant for Darius. 'But I've done obstacle courses worse than this in the dark. Don't worry about me. What's the plan?'

'I'll tell you after it's worked,' Darius said. He crouched and grabbed Constance's calves.

'Hey!' she said.

'Sorry in advance!' He stood up between her legs, with her thighs resting on his shoulders. She panicked and twisted at first, almost causing him to lose his balance, but he brought her close enough to a wall that she managed to brace them both. 'There's a ladder in front of you,' he said, groaning with exertion. 'Please grab it quickly.'

Constance flailed blindly for a few more knee-quivering seconds before her weight lifted from Darius's shoulders. Then she climbed like a monkey, all the sightless clumsiness gone as she rose. Darius hopped up after her, helping her get up the stairs. The armored robot was leaning forward, its various running lights dark, while the five regular infantry stumbled around like drunks.

They reached the last set of stairs before the roof, and Darius risked glancing down. The infantry had come to their senses. They looked up and trained their weapons on Darius and Constance.

'Hurry!' he yelled. There were enough layers of iron lattice between them and the ground to deflect most of the bullets—for now. But the sound of shattering glass and the ricochet of gunfire reminded Darius how very unsafe they were.

'How are your eyes?' Darius gasped as he helped Constance over the edge onto the roof.

'Getting better,' she said. 'They don't burn as much, and I can track movement, sort of. How big is this roof?'

Darius looked around and felt his stomach drop when he saw the other end of the rooftop less than fifty feet away. The next building was three stories taller. It did have another fire escape that he could probably reach with a running start, but there was no way Constance could make it in her current condition.

'I'm gonna be honest,' he said. 'Things don't look good.'

The fire escape began to clang and shake. Darius guessed that Ludd's soldiers would probably move slow—their heads would still be fuzzy from the grenade, and they'd had to leave their ace on the street. He figured he had about two minutes before he needed to be gone.

'Is there another way out?' she said. She leaned against the ledge and started rifling in her bag.

'There is,' Darius said. 'But . . .'

'But you would have to leave me behind,' Constance said softly.

'That's not happening!' Darius exclaimed.

'No,' she said. She stood up again, holding an entire belt of olive-green grenades. 'It's okay, Darius. This time, I have a plan of my own.'

'But this is suicidal!'

'This is the part where *you* trust *me*,' Constance said. 'And I need you to go, now, if that's all right. I . . . have to talk to someone, in private.'

'Okay,' Darius tried to say, but his throat was closing and he couldn't make any sound. He gave her a nod instead, and turned to run toward the opposite ledge.

'Hey, Malik?' he heard Constance say behind him. 'No, there's not much time. I just wanted to say—'

And then Darius jumped, his arms stretched out to grab the fire escape on the far wall. As he moved through the air, a wave of orange light crashed over him, followed by a white-noise roar that blotted out the whole world. The shock wave spun him around, and he collided with the fire escape instead of grabbing it. A lightning strike of pain slammed into him, rattling his bones, before he began to fall.

In a second that stretched into forever, Darius remembered the last time he saw his father. He was standing on the beach, watching Darius play in the waves. Darius turned to say something, to ask him to watch some silly trick, and a wave had slapped into him from behind, sending him tumbling, choking, too confused to scream, until he flopped down at his father's feet. His nose and his throat had hurt so much. His skin had been rubbed raw by the sand. But strong arms had picked him up from the beach and comforted him. He remembered his father smelling like sandalwood, and the scent expanded to fill Darius's entire body as he blacked out.

Chapter Nineteen

15:20 remaining

It was raining in London. Big Ben's loud *tick-tock* cut through the sound of the downpour, reminding Bianca that the clock was ticking on their twenty-four hours, that they had a little more than half their time left. She rubbed her hands up and down her arms, shivering from the chill. She could have waited in the car, but she'd wanted to come up here with Leon, just in case there was any resistance from Ludd's men. So far, though, Big Ben was completely empty.

If Leon minded the wet and the cold, he didn't show it.

He leaned out an open panel in Big Ben's huge face and tapped at his computer screen, lost in a world of his own. Water ran in little streams down his hair and from the tip of his nose.

'Is it all right for that thing to get wet?' Bianca's voice echoed in the open space at the top of the tower. Her mind began to unclench a little. It would be impossible to fly a helicopter or scale a brick wall in this weather, and she would hear anyone coming up the stairs. She took the opportunity to relax, stretching her arms out over her head.

Leon looked at her in surprise, as if he'd forgotten she was there. 'What?' he said. 'No, this thing's sealed tighter than a submarine. The back casing's even bulletproof.' His fingers kept working at the computer while he spoke, as though they had a mind of their own.

'You almost done? You need to get out of the rain. It's too cold up this high.'

'Yeah, almost done,' Leon said, executing a few more quick commands before flipping the computer into his pocket. The moment he stepped away from the window, he bent over shivering, like he'd suddenly become aware that he had a body. 'When did it get so c-cold?'

Bianca sighed and pulled off her cardigan, leaving her with nothing to ward off the cold but her damp tank top. The wet chill hit her immediately, but she was in much better shape than Leon and something told her she was going to work up a sweat soon anyway. She wrapped the sweater around Leon's neck and head, vigorously rubbing his arms as they walked back down the cramped spiral staircase.

'How can it be this cold?' he said, his teeth chattering. 'It's s-summer.'

'Doesn't matter,' Bianca said. 'It's raining. Maybe next time you'll make a sensor without a stupid design flaw like having to be high up, huh?'

'Hey, it's not like I had much time to work with.' Leon sneezed weakly. 'Thanks for the sweater.'

'No problem.' Bianca noticed that he was looking straight ahead, his cheeks suddenly pink. She rolled her eyes and pushed his shoulder, almost sending him tumbling down the stairs. 'Come on, dude, it's a tank top. We've been sparring for years, and I never wear more than a sports bra.'

'But you're also punching me in the head,' he said, then cracked a rare smile. 'Really, though, it doesn't matter what you're wearing. I could never think about you or Constance that way, you know? You're like my sisters.'

Bianca slowed down, putting her a few steps behind Leon so he couldn't see her look of surprise. 'We are?'

'I mean, I've never had siblings, so I'm not totally sure how they interact normally,' Leon said. 'I know we always give one another a hard time, but you guys are the only people I've ever respected.'

'Oh.' Bianca almost wanted to hug the idiot, but

something told her that would just make him more uncomfortable.

'Anyway,' he said, turning around to face her as they reached the bottom floor. Big Ben's imposing double doors were still cracked open, allowing a weak stream of light and a small pool of water into the room. 'Sorry for being all awkward. I promise I wasn't skeezing out on you or anything. I'm just not used to people being nice.'

A pleasant warmth rose into Bianca's chest and she stepped forward, forgetting any concerns about Leon's comfort, to wrap her arms tight around him. He froze for a second or two and then returned the hug. His hands were icy cold on her back, but she didn't care.

'Thanks,' Leon said, when she let him go.

'Don't tell anybody,' they both said, almost in unison, then burst out laughing.

The moment was interrupted by the sound of an engine revving. Bianca switched gears in an instant, running to kick open the door and bringing her handgun up defensively. Wind and rain blew into her face, blinding her for a moment. She blinked the water out of her eyes just in time to see their car driving off, spraying a puddle on a pair of unfortunate late-night pedestrians. Leon ran out into the street after her, a gun in his hand as well.

'Luddites?' he said.

Bianca growled and scanned up and down the street,

looking for any hint of white-and-black uniforms in the misty gray mess. She holstered her gun, screamed, and kicked over a nearby trash can.

'Thieves!' she screamed, turning to him with her arms spread wide.

'Did you lock the doors?' Leon rubbed his arms again.

'Of course I didn't lock the freaking doors!' She picked a piece of loose stone up from the sidewalk and stormed over to another nearby car. 'Why would it occur to me to lock the *door*? I didn't grow up in the real world, like you and Darius and everyone else!' She smashed the car's driver-side window, blinking back tears, and reached in to pull the door open from the inside.

'What are you doing?' Leon said. He was standing near the door, where the rain was a little lighter, giving Bianca the same look Darius had given her when she'd lost her temper in the sparring room.

'I need a drill,' she said, after a few deep breaths. Leon handed her a small electric hand drill and stood outside the car, a nervous expression on his face. 'Come on, Leon, get out of the rain before you get hypothermia.'

She unlocked the passenger door and opened it for him. He was shivering badly. Bianca pressed the drill against the ignition and turned it on, filling the car with the teeth-scratching sound of grinding metal. She felt the pins break after a few seconds and handed the drill to back to Leon.

'Screwdriver,' she said.

'What happened to pulling people out of their cars and driving off?' he tried to joke, handing her a long flat head screwdriver. His hand was shaking badly, and his teeth were chattering.

'I'm trying to grow as a person,' she said. She put the screwdriver in the ignition and turned it, and the engine sprang to life easily. Leon cranked up the heat and held his hands against the vents, sighing with relief.

'You're letting Darius get to you.'

'He knows things I want to know,' Bianca said, shooting a withering look at Leon. 'I'm not stupid enough to ignore that just because I don't like him.'

'Sure you don't,' Leon said flatly.

'Whatever. Where am I headed, anyway?'

'Piccadilly Circus.' Leon retrieved his computer and activated the GPS. 'It's less than two miles.'

Bianca put the car in drive and pulled out, following Leon's directions. It was a little awkward driving on the left side of the road, especially with standing water everywhere, but she had the streets to herself. The rainwater on the windows distorted the streetlights into a moving Impressionist painting, twirling and blending like Van Gogh's *Starry Night* come alive. Wind and rain tore through the broken window, but the car's heaters were enough to keep the chill at bay. The windshield wipers sloshed an even rhythm, forming a lullaby with the pounding rain. At moments like this, Bianca could almost forget who she was and why she was here.

Two blocks away from Piccadilly Circus, a swarm of bullets ripped through their car. The windshield shattered, spraying pebbles of safety glass into Bianca's and Leon's faces. Leon curled forward, placing his hands over his head protectively, bracing himself in his seat as Bianca slammed on the brake. The car's wheels had lost their grip on the road, and the car threatened to hit a streetlight. Leon screamed.

But instead of fighting the turn, Bianca accelerated into it, hitting the gas at just the right moment and narrowly dodging the streetlight at a full sixty miles an hour. As they spun away, she glanced in the rearview mirror and saw a dozen white-armored figures disappearing from the rooftops. Her sigh of relief caught in her throat as five white-and-black motorcycles roared out of the shadows behind them, their riders brandishing submachine guns.

'Duck!' Bianca screamed, slouching forward until all she could see were the tops of the buildings rushing past. Another round of bullets tore through the top of the seat, where her head had been mere moments before. Spinning the wheel violently, she swerved the car around, so that the approaching motorcycles were facing the driver's side of the car. Rain pelted her face through the broken windshield, stinging like hail. She winced, hoping this was the right move, and checked for her gun.

The nearest motorcycle swerved wildly to avoid her, sending its rider head first into the asphalt. A second crashed into the back of the car like a rag doll, with a bone-shattering crunch. His motorcycle spun into the path of a third rider's front tire, sending him flipping forward, driving his skull into the pavement. The last attacker rode on, narrowly avoiding the wreckage of his companions as he prepared to fire his weapon. Bianca snapped her own weapon up and fired at him. She missed him by a mile, but the bullets sparking against his motorcycle were enough of a distraction to make him crash into a nearby building.

'You can sit up,' Bianca said.

Taking a deep breath, she eased on the gas pedal and turned back toward Piccadilly Circus. The car wobbled as it moved, and there was a strange gurgle coming from the engine. The collision had probably warped the rear axle. But they only had a few blocks to go. She willed herself to drive normally, her eyes avoiding the rearview mirror.

'You scare me sometimes, you know?' Leon said. He ran his shaking hands through his wet hair and let out a long breath through chattering teeth.

'Only sometimes?'

By the time they reached Piccadilly Circus, the rain had died down, leaving a fog thicker than Bianca had ever seen. The intersection wasn't as brightly lit as Times Square had been, and the late hour meant it was almost completely abandoned, but there was a mixture of futuristic technology and Victorian architectural styles that made the art nerd inside her drool a little. Standing in the empty square, with the blinking advertisements directed only at her and Leon, Bianca felt like the world had become her own personal museum.

'I'm going to see if I can get a better read now that we're closer,' Leon pronounced. 'Keep an eye out?'

Bianca nodded, looking carefully in every direction, but there was no one around. She started to examine the billboards more carefully, wondering if the device could be behind another hidden door—when a loud burst of static exploded in her earpiece. She cried out and grabbed her ear. Leon looked up at her, his eyebrows raised.

'My radio,' she growled. 'I think it's broken.' She reached up to take it out, but Leon held up a hand, indicating that she slow down. He typed something on his computer; and almost immediately the static in Bianca's ear warbled and softened, until eventually a voice could be made out through the noise.

'I repeat,' a thick, Russian-accented voice said. 'Raise hand if you hear this message.'

Bianca and Leon exchanged a look of concern. Bianca tapped her earpiece, sending a transmission of her own.

'Who is this?'

'I repeat,' the voice said again. 'Raise hand if you hear this message.'

Bianca slowly raised her hand, her curiosity momentarily overcoming her caution.

'Ah!' the voice said, chortling with pleasure. 'Good, good. I apologize for confusion, but my radio has been made wet, and now it works not so good. Tell me, I see a boy and a girl below me, I think. Are you the Constance girl or the Bianca girl?'

'What the hell is happening?' Bianca whispered to Leon. Her stomach clenched in a sudden chill. 'He knew my *name*.'

'I don't know. But I don't think we should be out in the open.'

'Oh, no,' the man cried. 'Once again I am simpleton. Please, raise one arm if Constance is yourself, two if Bianca.'

Bianca decided to throw caution to the wind and raised both hands.

'*Fantasticheskiy!* I was afraid I would have to shoot you and be done. Is a boring idea. But Ludd has told me to look out for Bianca. I should very much like to fight you. I have not had fight worth speaking of for more than a decade.'

'Okay, so *all* of Ludd's hit men are certifiably insane,' Bianca mumbled.

'I am anxious for fight, so I will give you hint: Believe it or not, I am going to smash your bones like glass and watch city burn. Now come find me!'

Bianca and Leon moved under a nearby awning, their eyes darting nervously up to the buildings around them.

'Can we trust this maniac?' Leon wondered.

Bianca tried to think of what Darius would say. 'Well, he could have shot us and he didn't, which means he wants us alive, at least for now. It sounds like he's near the device—and even if he isn't, we need to know how he knows about us. So do we have a choice?'

'I guess not,' Leon said. 'What do you think about that hint, though?'

'He said he would snap our bones. Is there a museum near here, like with dinosaur skeletons?'

'That's just one part of the hint, though. What about the stuff about the city burning? What could that mean?'

Bianca rubbed her knuckles against her forehead and paced, trying to put all the pieces together. The clue had mentioned glass; but while there were a lot of glass windows in the storefronts surrounding her, none of them seemed promising. The famous fountain in the center of the inter-section had a statue of Cupid on top, but what did the god of love have to do with it? Could there be a fire station nearby that she had somehow missed?

It was probably right in front of her. She sighed and threw her head back, her gaze falling on one of the large, older-looking buildings. Its sides were bathed in purple-and-blue lights, and the fog made it hard to discern details, but the sign illuminating its front was crystal clear.

'Of course,' she said in her most deadpan voice. 'Ripley's Believe It or Not!'

167

'Okay. Now you *have* to kill him.'

'Let's get a move on, then,' Bianca agreed.

They crossed the plaza to the Ripley's building and spent a few minutes searching before they found the loading door. It was closed, with a heavy padlocked chain threaded between the handles.

'Good!' the voice said once they found the entrance. 'Not far now, *svetchke*. I look forward to breaking you!'

Leon raised an eyebrow at her. Bianca shrugged and rolled her eyes, trying to tamp down the knot of tension building up in her stomach. He pulled a pair of bolt cutters out of his satchel and made quick work of the chains.

'Really?' Bianca said.

'What?'

'Nothing.' She shrugged. 'Just seems a little low-tech for you.'

'When you find a way to hack into *chains* I'll be happy to hear.' He followed her up a promising-looking maintenance stairway. They made their way without resistance to the top, with Bianca on point, only to find another black cube sitting out in the open on the roof.

'Where is he?' Bianca muttered.

'Maybe he got distracted,' Leon said. 'Maybe attention deficit disorder just helped save the world.'

'No. He's around here somewhere.' Bianca was sure of it.

'Get to work, though. We'll deal with him when he shows himself.'

Leon shrugged and knelt beside the cube, retrieving his tools.

'How long will this take?' Bianca asked.

'A little longer than last time.' Leon rolled his glowing blue film back up and got out his toolkit. 'This one isn't a decoy, so it has some pretty good security measures inside.'

'But you can do it?' Bianca prodded. Leon gave her a withering look, and she raised her hands in surrender. 'Sorry, sorry, I never doubted you for a second.' She walked over to the edge of the balcony and looked down, but the street was hidden beneath a layer of fog. Even her clothes were damp with it, not that she had ever really dried off from the rain. She shivered and rubbed her hands over her arms, trying to warm them.

'Bianca!' Leon screamed behind her.

A lightning bolt shot down Bianca's spine as she turned. Running across the roof toward her was a man in the white armor of Ludd's soldiers. Where the woman on the subway had looked strangely normal, this man was the exact opposite. He had a short, wiry beard crisscrossed with extensive scarred, bald patches. His eyes were bright and steel gray, his face twisted into a grotesque mask of excitement.

Bianca directed three quick shots toward the man's center mass, accounting for his speed and the likely routes he would use to dodge. He made a loud *tsch* sound and leaped straight up, easily avoiding the bullets.

Bianca tossed her gun aside and sprinted. Out of the corner of her eye she saw Leon pick it up. She crashed into the man, sending them both rolling to the tiles a few feet away. The man snapped his legs toward Bianca, setting up a hold that might have broken half the bones below her waist, but she curled into a ball and kicked quickly into the air, landing in a crouch. Leon was standing now, aiming her gun at them with both hands, his arms shaking.

'Put the gun away,' she panted without taking her eyes from the man.

'What?'

Bianca bounced from foot to foot as the man slowly, deliberately got to his feet. He kept his head low and his shoulders forward. His nostrils flared and his eyebrows twitched, but otherwise his face was a mask of stone.

'You're just as likely to shoot me,' Bianca said slowly. 'You concentrate on your work. I'll concentrate on mine.'

'Listen to girlfriend,' the man interrupted. 'I kill you clean when she is gone, as long as you do not interfere, *da*?'

'I'm not his girlfriend.' Bianca presented her profile and held a hand out, in the universal gesture for 'Come at me.'

The man laughed that same murderer's chuckle and charged. She expected a tackle and a rib-crushing squeeze, but he twisted at the last minute, almost too late for Bianca to react to his feint. He drove his hand up, the fingers extended to act like a spear tip. She kicked his arm, wincing at the jarring, iron strength in it, and twirled around to his side.

'*Sambo*,' she breathed, as she peppered her attacker's torso with a flurry of punches and kicks. He blocked as many as he could, more than anyone but Bianca's instructors had ever managed, but her attack was fast and chaotic enough that he still gave ground. 'With a little bit of *Krav Maga*. Where'd you learn that?'

The man stopped retreating as they reached the edge of the roof. He smiled, though it looked more like a grimace because of all his scars. He pulled her close and twisted her into a hold that threatened to reverse both her elbows.

'You talk too much,' the man rasped into her ear. 'And you watch too many movies. Bruce Lee is dead.'

The rational corner of Bianca's brain struggled not to panic. Many of the people she fought were stronger than she was, and a few were even faster, but no one had ever been both. Still, he had one weakness she could take advantage of. She raised her leg and kicked as hard as she could into his crotch. Her foot twisted sickeningly as it encountered a solid armor plate. He howled in pain anyway, but remained standing.

Bianca hopped forward, praying she hadn't broken any bones in her foot. The man was doubled over, clutching at the spot where she had kicked him, but seemed to be recovering fast. She gingerly tried to put weight on her right foot and almost passed out from the pain. The man swam in and out of focus. Her eyes drifted to the void behind him, and she began to formulate an idea.

Bracing herself for a jolt of sheer agony, she ran forward and jumped. The man was still bent over as she lashed out with both legs, turning herself into a human battering ram. Both feet landed on his chest, launching him back into open space. Bianca's head swam with pain, but an overwhelming feeling of relief shot through her like adrenaline once he disappeared over the ledge.

She was about to stagger back toward Leon when the man's hand latched painfully onto her right ankle. Her stomach hit the ground and she started to slide backward, willing herself not to black out. She let out a guttural, throat-tearing howl of pain, her fingernails grasping for a hold on the smooth surface of the roof. But she just kept sliding.

For a split second, Bianca was weightless, suspended in the air—then a razor-sharp pain sliced through her hands as her desperate fingers latched onto a window frame. Her shoulders threatened to tear out of their sockets. The man's grip on her leg tightened and her vision swam.

'Let go of me!' she screamed. 'You're going to kill both of us!'

'That is the plan, yes,' the man growled.

He began to climb up her legs. She felt his other hand

squeeze around her knee, his grip threatening to snap her leg. That little bit of added pain was enough to break her focus for a moment, and her grip loosened. They both tumbled down the angled tiles on the outer edges of the roof. Her eyes closed, Bianca grabbed wildly at the surface, and managed to get her elbows hooked on a gutter.

The sudden stop shook the bearded man free, but he pulled hard as he dropped. Bianca heard the horrible cracking in her knee before she felt it. The colors and shapes of the world smeared again, like they had in the car. As a hand reached out to her from somewhere above, the only thought in Bianca's mind was the realization that she would never see the Sistine Chapel.

Chapter Twenty

11:25 remaining

In the back of his mind, Darius dimly registered that someone was yelling. His mom, maybe? He shook his head and groaned, trying to remember why his body was nothing but a tangle of angry, burning nerve endings.

Then the last few seconds rushed back to him, and he sat up straight, almost passing out again at the pain. How had he survived? He looked up at the four-story building he'd just tumbled from, and then down at the lumpy surface beneath him. He had landed in a truck bed full of pillows with large-eyed, colorful cartoons printed on them. He was in Tokyo. He was being chased by an insane ecoterrorist's armored robot, and a truckload of anime-printed pillows had just saved his life.

'Darius!' He winced at the volume of Malik's voice in his earpiece. 'Darius, come in! Oh God, please be alive. Darius!'

'M'here . . .' Darius croaked. He threw his legs over the truck bed and dropped to the street, almost collapsing from dizziness.

'Is Constance all right?' Malik asked wildly. Darius blinked and looked around. The building he had fallen from was left scorched and smoking, and most of the cars parked on the street had been smashed by flying rubble. Two bodies were crumpled on the sidewalk, and a third was embedded in a garbage truck's windshield. All three wore the tattered remains of Luddite uniforms.

'I'm not sure,' Darius said. 'I mean, she was right there in the explosion, so I don't . . . I'm not sure how she could have survived that.'

Before he could fully process Constance's fate, Darius heard the sound of gunfire from down the street, where a sickeningly familiar eight-foot-tall figure was stomping around the corner. A dozen police officers were shooting at it from behind the cover of their car doors. A panel popped up on the armor's right shoulder as the whining sound rose again; and then a shot of flame released from the panel, leaving one of the squad cars a melted hulk.

Darius's determination to see the mission through, back in New York, seemed unbelievably childish now. What did any of that mean, in the face of this monstrosity? His leg muscles tensed, instinctively primed to flee.

But then Constance's goodbye to Malik echoed in his ear, shaming him into action. He ran and grabbed one of the dead Luddites' discarded rifles, bracing it against his shoulder the way Malik had showed him, and squeezed the trigger. A stream of bullets exploded out, cascading so many sparks across the armored machine's frame that it seemed to glitter. The clip ran out with a series of clicks and slowly, its footsteps thudding angrily, the armored robot turned and fixed its red eye on Darius.

Darius dropped the gun and sprinted for a park across the street, cutting a straight line through the brush. The robot had been designed for open city streets, and he hoped that the dense growth might slow it down. His lungs stung, still recovering from the impact of his fall, and he tripped a few times as he ran, half-blinded by the leaves slapping at his face. But the sounds of tearing and snapping in the trees behind him were getting steadily closer. He doubted he had more than a minute before the thing caught up to him, and then it would be over.

Then, over the nightmarish sounds from the machine behind him, Malik's voice breaking through the static in his ear, and his own labored breathing, Darius heard something else. The piercing howl of a train's whistle. It gave him an idea.

Darius took a deep breath and exploded back out of the trees into the street, jumping onto the hoods of nearby cars in a single leap and sliding over their roofs on the seat of his pants. The robot was still behind him, its feet echoing on the concrete, but he couldn't stop to look. His only hope was to keep running.

Finally, Darius turned the corner and saw a set of train tracks running below a raised part of the street a few yards away. Another whistle cut through the air—a train was coming soon. Darius ran onto the overpass and turned, crouching low to the ground. The bridge didn't look very sturdy, and the armored robot had to weigh at least a ton. Surely the bridge wouldn't hold, and the robot would tumble down onto the train below.

But the robot started moving toward him—and the ground didn't break. Darius realized with a sinking feeling that his plan wouldn't work. He turned to run, but there was no cover here and he was too tired. It felt like he was at the bottom of a deep pool, the light miles above his head, his limbs answering his commands sluggishly if at all. The thunder of the armored robot's footsteps echoed in his bones. He felt something close around his torso and lift him up. It was the robot's unbreakable metal fist.

He kicked his feet wildly, screaming at the top of his lungs as the arm lowered him over the side of the over-pass, to hang suspended in the middle of the tracks.

A wind kicked up from the direction of the tunnel, pulling teasingly at Darius's legs while the sound of the train rattled deep down in his teeth and his gut. He kicked and twisted, clawing at the arm, almost tearing away his fingernails as he tried to remove its grip, but the thing didn't even budge. The train was coming and would hit his body with all the force of a huge metal object traveling at 180 miles an hour.

He closed his eyes, bracing himself for the impact. At least he would die instantly.

Then there was a screech above him, and the sound of a single bullet firing, and the arm pulled him quickly back up to the street. Darius felt the train's slipstream catch his foot, the train itself missing him by inches. The robot's claw released him, and he tumbled to the ground. Crawling on hands and knees, gasping for breath, Darius scrambled away. He didn't know what game the robot was trying to play with him—maybe Ludd wanted to literally drive him crazy, to break him—but at least he wasn't dead this very minute.

'Hey!' a familiar, bubbly voice broke through his thoughts. 'What has two thumbs and just saved Tokyo?'

Darius turned around. His vision swam with tears, but he could just make out Constance, her skin alternatingly black with soot or painfully raw and pink, her long blond hair singed off in places, sitting on the armor's left shoulder, swinging a handful of exposed wires.

'This girl!' she said, pointing at herself and grinning.

Chapter Twenty-One

05:42 remaining

The plane's engines droned steadily, reminding Bianca of the air vent above her bed back home. Her eyelids drooped, and she shook her head. She never should have accepted Leon's painkillers. She remembered complaining to Malik about her trouble sleeping and his suggestion that she put white noise on her speakers. She'd tried the sound of thunderstorms, only to realize that she hadn't witnessed an actual thunderstorm first-hand since she was recruited. But this soft buzzing, and the fuzzy feeling of warmth flowing up from her anesthetized leg, were enough to drill through even her insomnia.

'Just let yourself sleep,' Leon said. Bianca shook her head again. Leon had been tapping away at his handheld computer for an hour, working on another of his arcane tech projects to pass the time. Now he was staring at her with his engineer's eyes, in a way that made her feel like he could see right through her. 'You need rest.'

'Need to stay alert,' Bianca mumbled.

He shrugged and went back to his computer.

'The rest of the team is about an hour out from San Francisco, by the way,' he said.

'They survived?'

'Apparently. Malik says Constance won't shut up about how jealous I'm going to be when I see her new toy.'

'What about Darius?'

Leon raised an eyebrow, and Bianca felt heat rise to her cheeks. She wanted to punch him, but she couldn't find the energy to lift her arm, let alone walk over.

'Shut up,' she said. 'He's my responsibility.'

'He's fine,' Leon said. He turned his attention back to his computer for a silent moment and then spoke again, without raising his eyes. 'You're not doing anything wrong, you know.'

'What?' Bianca murmured from her drowsy trance.

'He's . . . well, he's not as smart as you are, at least not book-smart,' Leon said. 'But he's street-smart, and funny. And not to be weird, but he's definitely good-looking.' He pursed his lips and held his stylus in the air for a few seconds, preoccupied with some nagging thought. 'And it's been months since—'

'Don't,' Bianca said flatly. She turned in her chair and curled up, leaning her head against the armrest. She opened her mouth, trying to think of a threat she could add to the warning, but sleep overtook her.

In her dreams, a sad-looking man and woman watched her life on television. They watched as a little girl with a black eye and scuffed knuckles sat cross-legged in an armory, playing music on a bulky military radio. The volume was turned up so loud that nobody could hear her cry, especially herself. But then a young man came in, a tuxedo made of shadows wrapping around him as he approached her. He was tall and thin, with messy red hair and a smile so brave it could laugh at death. He took the girl's hand, and suddenly it was the hand of a Bianca who didn't wake up screaming. In her dreams they danced, circling past the racks of guns and the lockers stuffed with armor, a dress made of stars swirling around her ankles as they spun.

Then the music stopped and the young man disappeared, leaving his smell on her pillow. The shadows pulled away, leaving Bianca in a white, empty room, with no doors, no clothes, and no soft edges.

The *whoosh* of the plane's door opening woke her. She shot straight up, her cheeks wet with tears and her hair a wild, tangled mess.

'Told you that you needed the rest,' Leon said, slinging his bag over his shoulder as he stood. 'The others are waiting.'

Bianca quickly wiped her face on a napkin and stretched. Her knee was an angry red color and painfully swollen, and she winced as she walked gingerly down the stairs. She followed Leon into another hangar, this one smaller than the one in JFK. Constance and Malik were seated in a pair of folding chairs a few yards away, next to something huge concealed under a tarp.

'That'll be her new "toy,"' Leon said, rolling his eyes. Bianca didn't say anything, just redid her hair into a high ponytail as she walked slowly over to their teammates. Constance looked pretty rough. Her uniform was scorched all over, and what was left of her formerly long, beautiful hair was frizzy and discolored. She stood and smiled as they approached though, whipping the tarp off with a flourish to reveal an eight-foot-tall robot patterned in the Luddites' white and black. Leon stood in place, his eyes and mouth slowly widening. Bianca shook her head and pushed past him.

'I knew it!' Constance said, slapping her hands together and pointing at Leon. 'Look at him. *Jealous!*'

'Leon told us about your injury,' Malik said to Bianca,

nodding down at her leg. He gave her a pained smile and took a sip from a paper cup. 'Welcome to the club.'

'Yeah,' Bianca said. Her head was still fuzzy from sleep, but she was awake enough for her body to remember how hungry it was. 'Is that coffee?'

'Yup.' Malik pointed to a door at the other end of the hangar. 'There's a kitchenette that way.'

'How much time do we have left?' she said.

'Six hours,' Malik reminded her. She nodded. Three devices in eighteen hours wasn't too shabby. They just needed to find the one in San Francisco, destroy it, and then get home. She gasped in pain again and leaned briefly against the doorframe for support. In her case, easier said than done.

The kitchenette was barely the size of one of their dorms, with a refrigerator, a microwave, a coffee pot, and a sink situated next to a small, dirty window. The details were fuzzed out by the glass, but she could still see San Francisco's lights burning in the distance, past the airfields. Darius looked up as she came in.

'Hi,' Bianca said.

'Hey.' He lifted a steaming paper cup and nodded at her. 'There's sandwiches in the refrigerator and coffee if you drink it.'

'Do you have anything stronger?' Bianca asked, trying to keep herself from wincing at the pain as she sat next to him.

'I could shoot at you,' Darius said. 'That's done a pretty good job of keeping *me* alert, so far.'

'I've built up a resistance,' she said, rubbing her temples. 'Coffee and a sandwich it is, then.'

Darius tossed her a plastic-wrapped triangle. She tried to open it casually but her hunger got the better of her, and she ended up stuffing half the sandwich into her mouth in a single bite. She hadn't realized until now how hungry she was.

'I'm starving,' she said as she reached across the table for another sandwich.

'Yeah, I noticed.' Darius took another sip of coffee. 'You sure can pack it down.'

'I have a fast metabolism.'

'You're incredibly active.' He nodded to her knee. 'I'm sorry about your injury. Must really suck.'

'Hey, watch yourself. One pity party was enough. Another might get you on the bench with me and Mal.'

'With you down a leg, I might just be able to take you,' he teased.

'I don't think so.'

'You're probably right,' he said, chuckling. 'Remember how bad you punked me when I first got recruited?'

'Sorry about that.' Bianca winced.

'It was an important lesson. Did you see that robot thing Constance brought back?'

She smiled. 'Leon looked like he wanted to cry when she ripped the tarp down.'

'We wouldn't have survived that fight if you hadn't beaten some humility into me.'

'Well, I'm glad you're okay,' she said quietly. There was a moment of silence, then Bianca remembered what she had wanted to tell him. 'Oh, and guess what? I hot-wired a car in London! You'd have been so proud.'

'You hot-wired a car *and* drove on the left-hand side of the street? I am proud!' The coffee machine beeped, and Darius moved to pour Bianca a cup.

'What's it like?' she asked finally, swirling her coffee without taking a sip.

'What's what like?'

'Being a—whatever you did before you were recruited.'

'A hustler?' he said. 'Grifter? Con artist?'

'Sure. I mean . . .' She trailed off. 'Did you know I was recruited when I was ten?'

'No, I didn't.'

'Malik said something before we left New York. He said that you guys had all lost your real lives, and your futures, and that since Oberon was pretty much the only life I'd ever known, I couldn't understand what I was asking the rest of you to give up by extending the mission.'

'I'm surprised,' Darius said. 'That was pretty insensitive of him.'

'You don't agree?'

'Nobody can ever know how someone else struggles,' he said.

'That's actually really insightful.'

'Knowing what makes people tick is what separates a grifter from a mugger.' He looked up at the ceiling. 'That and imagination.'

Bianca laughed and brushed a strand of hair behind her ear. 'But really, tell me what it was like.'

'Lonely,' he said. Bianca cocked her head, curious. He sighed and went on. 'You gotta think of everybody else as marks. Everybody separates the world into me versus them a little bit, but when you're a con artist, it's all black and white. The only people who aren't marks are the people you care about and the people too dangerous to touch, and you don't want the first to find out what you do or the second to dump your body in a river, so you can never trust anyone. You're alone.'

'Parents?'

'My dad wasn't a bad guy,' Darius said, rubbing his forehead. 'But he only knew how to live one kind of way, and that's what he taught me. I think Mom hated him for that, but she's been gone for a few years now too. It's hard to remember either of them with any detail anymore.'

'I know what you mean,' Bianca said softly. 'My parents gave me up when I was a little girl. I used to be sick all

187

the time. It was just too much for them to handle.' She hugged herself. 'Sorry, I shouldn't have brought any of this up. I guess I thought . . . I don't know, that the way you lived was somehow *fun*.'

'It was, sometimes,' Darius agreed. 'It was always fun to set the mark up so they could show you they were a bad person. It made it feel less like crime. Like this one time a guy on a corner tried to sell me some fake watches. Now usually I don't touch poor folks or other workers, but this guy was a little too aggressive about his pitch, and he got on my nerves.'

'How did you prove he was a bad person?'

Darius chuckled. 'I told him I really wanted a Rolex for the prices he was offering, but I needed the money to help my mom buy her medicine. He kept pushing, so I felt justified lifting his wallet. And then there was the guy I took the same day I was recruited. He was a total out-of-towner. Hawaiian-shirt-sportin', sandals-with-socks-wearin', frosted-tips-on-top-of-300-pounds-havin' poser. I set up a table like I was running a three-card monte game, which is where—'

'I'm familiar with the concept,' Bianca said.

'Everyone is,' Darius continued. 'Which is why it's useless as a con. But a lotta people don't know that everybody else in the world knows about it, so I thought of a fun trick. I made this guy feel like we were buds, and then I had a friend of mine come by, and we let this guy think he was stealing my friend's money while we cleaned him out.'

Bianca smiled at the thought. 'That's pretty clever.'

'Nah.' Darius waved a hand dismissively. 'Nothing special about a double-cross, I just put my own spin on it.'

Bianca thanked him for cheering her up and excused herself. Leon and Constance were still arguing, in their almost incomprehensible techie version of English, when she went back to the hangar.

'Your qualifications are meaningless,' Leon said. 'Have you factored air friction into your algorithm?'

'I've already piloted it!' Constance exclaimed.

'Everybody shut up,' Bianca interrupted. 'Ludd doesn't care how many episodes of *Star Trek* you've seen. Time to go.'

Chapter Twenty-Two

03:15 remaining

Darius pulled his jacket closed, trying to block the cold wind blowing in from the Pacific. The others stood at the railing of the Golden Gate Bridge, looking out over the mirror-bright bay and the city beyond while they waited for Leon to climb back down from one of the bridge's giant struts.

'What's taking him so long?' Darius asked.

'He's afraid of heights,' Bianca said, leaning out over the void. 'Just relax. He would've radioed us if he was stuck, and if he'd fallen we would know. This is his own fault, for not trusting any of the rest of us with his computer.'

'Relax?' Malik said. 'Are you still high on painkillers or something? We have only a few hours left and no idea where the final device is!'

'I don't know.' Bianca shrugged. 'I've just got this feeling.'

Darius looked sidelong at Bianca. She was leaning against the rail next to him, her gaze firmly locked out on the water.

'What kind of feeling?' he demanded.

Her eyes flicked to his and quickly moved away again. 'I feel like Ludd's not stupid enough to let the same trick work four times in a row. Our odds are pretty bad. We may not be able to complete this mission, guys.'

The sparse, late-night traffic and the roar of the ocean filled the next few moments, before their earpieces clicked to life and Leon's voice came through.

'I've got bad news,' he said.

A van stopped a few yards away from them, its engine idling.

'What is it?' Bianca asked Leon, but her eyes were locked on Darius. Her voice was flat and her expression distant.

'I can't get a lock,' Leon said. 'I'm picking up the same energy signatures as before, but something's jamming us. Maybe we're just too far away.'

Traffic started backing up behind the van. Malik and Constance looked up as people began honking.

'That's weird,' Malik said. He reached for his gun and narrowed his eyes, but Constance put a hand on his wrist.

The van's side door opened, and seven Luddites streamed out, their weapons pointed at the four teammates. Darius turned to run, his heart slamming against his aching ribs, only to see another white van come to a stop on the other side of the bridge. Bianca grabbed his jacket from behind and pulled him close.

'Everyone put your hands up,' Bianca hissed. She looked around, scowling as Darius and the others refused to move. 'Now!'

Darius jumped and shot his hands into the air, trying to keep them from shaking. He looked at Bianca. Her hands were still in her pockets. She had turned away from the ocean, but she was still staring into the middle distance.

Bianca raised her voice to address the Luddites. 'I have a proposal!'

The Luddites stayed silent for a long time, looking back and forth between one another.

'What are you *doing*?' Darius exclaimed. The wind picked up, whipping Bianca's hair around and reminding him of how she'd looked on the Empire State Building, like some kind of terrible warrior princess.

'Shut up,' Bianca snapped. Her mouth hardened into a razor-straight line, and her gaze never left the empty space in front of her.

Malik fixed her with a stare that could have frozen the sun. Constance bit her knuckles.

'What is your offer?' one of the men said, his voice so heavily modulated by the speakers in his helmet that he sounded to Darius like a demon.

'I can help your boss. Take me to him.'

The man directed his gun at Bianca. 'I'm sorry, but I don't think I trust you, not after you've killed so many of our forces.'

'You need proof that I'm serious?' Bianca's voice hardened.

Suddenly, a sound of metal tapping rang out from above, and an oblivious Leon dropped into the middle of the bridge.

'All right,' Leon said, grunting. 'Any new ideas? I'm thinking that maybe—*oh.*' His eyes widened as he took in the scene around him.

'Bianca,' Leon said, slowly. 'You've got a plan, right?'

'I do,' Bianca said. She turned on her heel and whipped out her pistol viper-fast, firing once into Leon's chest. Leon fell like a rag doll to the ground. Constance doubled over and screamed. Darius tried to remember how to breathe as a red-hot ball of rage formed in his chest.

'I'm tired of this crap,' Bianca announced. 'Of putting everyone else's lives before mine. Of working myself to death for the people who stole my childhood, so that I can protect a world that will never even know about me. I'm done.'

'You monster!' Constance screamed. Her cheeks were shiny with tears. 'Murderer! Liar!'

'Shut. UP!' Bianca said. Her eyes were wide. She turned the gun on Constance. Her chest heaved but she kept her aim steady. She was a professional, after all.

'That's enough,' Ludd's head soldier said, apparently listening to the commands of someone in his earpiece. 'Drop your weapon, and enter the van with your hands up.'

'On one condition,' Bianca said. 'You leave the rest of them alive.'

'Why should we?'

'Because they're useless without me, and I won't help you if you kill them.'

'Fine,' the man said after a moment.

Bianca limped over to the van and pulled herself halfway in. She turned and fixed an angry, tired look on them.

'It's been *fun*,' she said sarcastically, and Darius felt for a moment that she was looking directly at him. 'Now go home.'

And she disappeared into the van. The Luddites followed her, and a few seconds later both vehicles were squealing away, a flood of newly freed traffic following them. Darius numbly wondered how long they had until police arrived.

They waited a few seconds in stunned silence, until Leon curled in on himself and started coughing.

'He's alive!' Constance cried out. She rolled Leon over on his back. He didn't appear to be bleeding, but there was a thumb-sized scorch mark above his heart.

'Oh my God, is that smoke?' Malik wondered aloud. A shower of sparks cascaded from Leon's chest, sending the others scrambling back.

'Leon's a robot!' Darius pulled out his gun and aimed it shakily at the prone form.

'I'm not . . . a robot.' Leon coughed. He leaned up on his elbows. 'You moron.'

'Why aren't you dead then?'

'Bulletproof computer.' Leon reached into his pocket and tossed a twisted piece of chrome and shattered plastic on the ground next to him.

'What do we do now?' Constance asked. Darius realized she and Malik were both looking at him.

'Kill Bianca,' Leon gasped, trying to get to his feet. Constance helped him up.

'There's more important things than revenge right now, man,' Darius said.

'*She . . . shot . . . me*,' Leon snarled, and there was a sulfurous rage in his eyes that gave Darius pause.

'Fine,' Darius said. The far end of the bridge lit up with flashing blue lights. Darius wondered what would happen if he just told the police everything—that he was a time-traveling crime fighter sent back through a portal to outwit a bunch of terrorists. Instead he squared his shoulders, turned, and walked back with the others in the direction of the hangar.

Chapter Twenty-Three

02:30 remaining

'You're awake,' a voice said from the darkness. It was cold and urbane, but a little rough around the edges, and sounded frighteningly familiar. Bianca groaned and opened her eyes. Ludd's face coalesced out of the blur, his lips pursed. 'I hope you aren't too uncomfortable.'

'You drugged me.'

'I didn't,' he said, raising himself back to his full height and adjusting his jacket. 'I had someone else do it.'

She sat up, slowly, and gave herself a visual check followed by a pat-down. She was still in her own clothes, and they had let her keep her weapons.

'I'm still armed,' she pointed out.

'My soldiers follow me out of admiration and trust,' Ludd told her. 'I am the great hunter of my tribe, you see? What message would I send my followers if I had to declaw an already lamed kitten?'

'This looks like a prison.' She tried to ignore his terrible description of her. The room they were in was small, made of rough-hewn stone. There was only one door, on the opposite side of the room from her. But the furnishings were strangely plush and expensive-looking, possibly antiques. She had vague memories of visiting her grandparents' house when she'd been little, before Oberon. This place reminded her of that.

'The only difference between a prison and a fortress is which way the guards face.'

'And you drugged me,' Bianca repeated, sitting up with one leg tucked under and her injured leg stretched out. Her hair had fallen in her face. She reached onto her wrist for a rubber band to tie it back up, but couldn't find one. She settled with pushing it behind her ears.

'Well,' Ludd said, smiling again. 'You *did* defeat Matvei in single combat. Bravery is not stupidity.'

'Whatever you say.'

'Indeed. Now, my men tell me you have an offer. I would like to discuss this. Can you walk on that leg?'

Bianca glared at him and stood, forcing herself not to grimace when she put weight on her injured limb.

'Brava,' he said. 'Follow me. We'll talk business in my command center.'

They walked out into a narrow hallway made of the same stone as the cell. Ludd kept his back to her, walking at just brisk enough a pace that she had to struggle to keep up.

'Where are the guards?' she asked.

'I have no personal guard.' He waved a hand carelessly. 'This plan was set in motion hours ago, and now I am little more than a figurehead. It would be tragic if I died, but even if you killed me now, the EM resonator would still go off, and everything would proceed as it must.'

'You sure are confident for somebody who's been beaten three times in a row by teenagers.'

He laughed. They walked into an open, slightly more modern-looking cell block, with dozens of white-armored men marching back and forth along the catwalks. They all turned and snapped to attention at Ludd's arrival.

'Stand down,' he said, projecting his voice without seeming to yell. The guards all relaxed and went back about their work. Ludd led her into a white-walled room slightly larger than the cell. It might have been a warden's office once, but instead of furniture there were dozens of computers and monitor arrays, some even showing areas she recognized. One displayed Times Square, another an aerial view of Piccadilly Circus in London, and a third a dense urban area that must have been Tokyo. Ludd sat in the room's biggest chair and turned to face her, steepling his fingers.

'The cell you woke up in,' he said. 'It was Al Capone's, when he was alive. Do you know of him?'

'I've seen the mobsters on *Looney Tunes*.'

'Indeed.' Ludd gave her a wry smile. 'I put you there to demonstrate a point, you know. Can you guess what that might be?'

'Not really, no,' Bianca said flatly.

'History remembers Al Capone as a thug with pretensions to aristocracy, but the working poor of Chicago thought differently. Mr. Capone was hated by the owning classes and legislators of the time because of the threat he represented to their power, and because he protected the poor from their greed. Villains are often no more brutal or villainous than heroes—the only difference is that the villain loses, and the hero gets to write history.'

'Except you're a mass murderer, and I'm not.'

'Mass murderer, perhaps not; but your body count is *staggeringly* high. And the nation you represent, ah, that is another story. What about the institution of slavery? The Trail of Tears? Manifest destiny? Hiroshima and Nagasaki? The list goes on. What are you if not the tool of mass murderers worse than I could ever be?'

'The examples you listed are all from history. And none of it compares with what you're doing.'

'You're deluding yourself. Would you be more comfortable with my work if I kidnapped young girls and turned them into killing machines?'

Bianca remained silent.

'Have you ever read *City of God*?'

'No,' Bianca said.

'There is a relevant passage in which Saint Augustine recounts a meeting between Alexander the Great and a pirate his men have captured. Alexander, speaking from the same position of delusional moral authority your keepers cleave to, asks the pirate what he means by claiming possession of the sea by force. The pirate responds, "What do you mean by seizing the whole Earth; but because I do it with a petty ship, I am called a robber, while you who do it with a great fleet are styled emperor." I am neither pirate nor emperor, Bianca.'

'I have a question for you,' Bianca said. 'Before I make my offer, I mean.'

He opened his hands, beckoning her to continue.

'What's your real motive?'

'A radically redefined social paradigm where technological progress is used to integrate man with his environment, where social progress is used to lift up the poor rather than exalt the wealthy.'

'So you use high technology and the mass killing of urban populations, most of whom are going to be poor, to build a new world of low technology and dignity for the poor?'

There was a long moment of silence, filled with faint radio static.

'You would prefer I organized a fun run, perhaps?' he said, the deepening lines on his face belying his composure. 'Other methods have been tried and found wanting. If I must injure Earth to save it from annihilation, then so be it.'

'I want evidence that you aren't a hypocrite. That you're not secretly in it for the money.'

'Would it help you to know that I liquidated my assets to fund this venture? My net worth currently rests in the single digits. But even as a pauper I think I can offer you what you want most of all. Your freedom.'

Her fists clenched. 'So you *do* have a way,' she said. 'I thought you might.'

'I can free you from Oberon easily. As you may have guessed from the form of the EM resonators—not to mention the timing of my attacks—you aren't the first of Oberon's agents to come to me. The question becomes, then, what can you do for me in return?'

'Anything,' Bianca said quickly. 'I will do anything if you can give me my freedom.'

'Good,' Ludd said. 'There's a lot I want to know about your masters—your former masters, now. But all those things in time. For now, let us enjoy the last few moments of life in this corrupt city.'

He turned the chair so that his back was to her. Bianca dropped the earpiece to the ground and quietly crushed it under her heel.

Chapter Twenty-Four

02:20 remaining

There was a long moment of silence once the signal cut out. Malik and Constance looked down at their laps while Leon scowled and typed furiously on a laptop he'd found in a locked supply cabinet. The kitchenette's single fan whirled slowly overhead while the sky darkened with late-afternoon shadows. Something about what Bianca had said clung to Darius's mind insistently, though he couldn't quite figure out what it was.

'Why would she do this?' Constance murmured. 'It's . . .

suicidal! She'll be erased at the cutoff, just like—'

'Just like Isaac,' Malik finished for her. 'I should have seen this coming.'

'What do we do now?' Constance asked, looking back and forth between Malik and Darius. 'We still don't even know where the device is!'

'Yes, we do.' Darius leaned forward eagerly. 'It's on Alcatraz.'

'What makes you say that?'

'Ludd mentioned Al Capone's cell. Capone was kept in Alcatraz.'

'How do you know that?' Malik asked curiously.

'Come on.' Darius shook his head. 'He was the *original* original gangster. But it doesn't make any sense. Alcatraz is pretty far out, isn't it? He won't get much of the city from there.'

'That's assuming that Ludd hasn't improved the yield,' Constance said nervously.

'I guarantee he has,' Leon said.

'No, you *guess* so,' Malik interrupted. 'We're in the dark about too many things. I say we leave.'

'Leave?' Darius's voice caught dangerously.

'I agree,' Constance offered.

'But our mission—'

'Our mission was completed hours ago,' Malik snapped. 'London and Tokyo were reckless gambles, but pushing forward now would be *insane*. We've already saved millions of people. That sounds like a success to me.'

'But we could save more!'

'Why? Who are they to me? Everyone is the focus of their own story, and everyone fears death, but *I* am the sole caretaker of my life.' Malik sighed, and his voice grew calmer. 'We are too valuable to Oberon to risk our own lives when there's no hope of success.'

'But there is hope!' Darius said. 'We've already accomplished the impossible on this mission. We can do it again.'

'We can't, actually,' Leon said, tapping one final key. He turned the display so they could all see what looked like a black-and-green aerial map of San Francisco.

'What am I seeing here?' Darius said.

'A map of our active doors in the Bay Area.'

'But I don't see anything.'

'Exactly,' Leon said with a sigh. 'Somehow, Ludd shut them down all across the West Coast. The nearest active door is in Chicago.'

'We barely have enough fuel to make the trip,' Constance cried.

'Not to mention *time*.' Malik stood up and started pacing back and forth, wincing at the pain in his thigh. 'What are we looking at now? Three hours?'

'Less than two and a half,' Leon said.

Darius chewed his lip. He noticed his hands were shaking.

He closed them and took a deep breath. 'You mentioned throwing your life away, Malik.'

'I did.'

'Bianca told me what you said back in New York, about how she didn't know what a real life was, because all of us had had our futures taken away.'

'How does anything she said matter now? She's a traitor.'

'It matters because you're a hypocrite,' Darius said. Malik gave him the sort of withering look he was used to seeing on Bianca, but he forged on. 'We had our lives taken from us, sure, but that doesn't mean we can't still *do* something with them. How many "normal" missions do you really think you can survive? How many people live as long as Agent Grosz?'

The other three looked away, unable to meet his gaze.

'Chances are we're going to die anyway. It's a numbers game, and I can tell you from experience that the only way to win a gamble is to cheat. So it's your choice how it happens. But as for me, I'm going to make my life worth as much as I can.' He paused and looked out the window, still trying to figure out what it was that Bianca had said that was needling him. 'Plus . . . I haven't given up hope on Bianca.'

'What? Why?' Constance exclaimed.

'She let us hear that conversation.'

'Could have been an accident,' Malik said. 'Or she could

have been letting us know how little hope there is. She did tell us to go home, remember?'

'Does Bianca ever do anything by accident? Anyway, I just have this . . . this *feeling* that she's still on our side. And if she's willing to give up everything to save this city, then why not all of us?'

'You're right,' Constance said. She stood up and joined Darius, squaring her shoulders. He put a hand on her arm and gave her a quick smile when he felt the slight tremble she was hiding.

'No,' Leon said. 'He isn't. And I'm not coming.'

'Yes, you are.' Malik shrugged. 'Constance and I are the only ones here who can fly the jets in that hangar.' He smiled at Leon's expression of shocked disbelief, then turned to Darius. 'I assume you have a plan.'

Darius looked pointedly at the deactivated powered armor. 'Sort of,' he said.

'You're sure you can do it?' Leon had to yell to be heard over the roaring wind from the plane's open doors. Malik was flying them low on the approach to the island, but the air was still biting cold, making it difficult to breathe.

'Yes,' Constance said, safely ensconced inside the massive robot armor. She flexed the machine's three-clawed hands.

'It's a really important job, though,' he said. 'If you don't take out all the external defenses we won't stand a chance.'

'Like we stand a chance anyway.'

'But—'

'That's enough,' Malik said from the cockpit. 'Cut the chatter.'

'Wonderful,' Leon said, flopping onto the bench next to Darius. 'I'm about to die and I don't even get to pilot a giant robot first.'

'If it makes you feel any better,' Darius said, 'I've never . . . you know.'

'None of us have,' Leon said. His mouth was a straight, thin line. He looked down at his hands and opened them slowly. 'Not a big dating scene back at the base.'

'Speak for yourselves,' Constance said. Darius and Leon gave her a long stare, their eyebrows climbing higher. 'What?'

'I could have,' Darius mused. 'There was this girl, Zoe . . .'

He paused for a moment and thought about the word he'd used. *Was*. Past tense. Had he said that because he was about to die? Or if he was being honest with himself, had he let go of Zoe the moment he stepped into the white van with Agent Grosz?

'She was special,' he went on, 'and we were so young. I thought we had our whole lives together, so I just . . . we wanted to wait until things were perfect.'

'Has this world been so kind to you that you should leave it with regret?' Malik said over the PA. 'There are better things ahead than any we leave behind.'

The speaker went silent. The only sounds were the faint buzzes of the armor's balancing systems reacting to the plane's movement, and the wind from outside. Darius wondered if he was supposed to cry, or if his life would flash before his eyes. But instead he just felt empty. He tried to imagine what was about to happen to him in forty-five minutes, when the clock ran out. Would he just pop out of existence like a soap bubble? Melt into nothingness?

'Fifteen seconds,' Malik said. Darius and Leon stood and straightened their parachutes as the ten-second countdown began.

'Good luck,' Darius said. Five seconds left.

'Thanks,' Constance said. Four seconds. 'I'm glad we met, Darius.'

'You're really not a virgin?' Leon asked, with two seconds left. 'It wasn't Malik, was it?'

'No, and shut up,' Constance said, but she was smiling as she pulled at the controls. The scarred, battered machine leaped from the side of the plane, the massive shift in weight knocking Darius and Leon to the floor. There was a thud from below as the armor landed in the prison's outer court-yard, and then the sound of machine gun fire and explosions overpowered the wind and the engines. Orange and red light flashed against the plane's windows.

'I'd say their outer defenses are officially dealt with,' Malik said. He locked in the plane's course and stood up, shouldering a parachute. Darius and Leon joined him. Darius had expected Leon to balk at the jump, but Leon surprised him by hopping out silently and without complaint. 'This is going to hurt my leg,' Malik said ruefully, before following him.

Darius walked to the door. He had another few seconds before the plane passed too far over the island. Even now, after everything he'd said at the hangar, a little voice in his head urged him to hop in the pilot's chair. How hard could flying be, after all? Leon had left the laptop with the door map open in the copilot's seat. He was a smart enough guy; surely he could figure out how to get to Chicago.

He shook his head and jumped, leaving the Darius who thought those kinds of thoughts back in the plane, to hopefully drown with it in the Pacific.

The heat from the fires down in the courtyard pushed angrily at his parachute, threatening to lift him and throw him into the sea. He curled his legs under him and gritted his teeth, pulling desperately. His feet just barely skimmed one of the outer fences, and he hit the ground so hard he was afraid he might have cracked a rib. He stood up gingerly, looking around at the courtyard, which was filled with piles of steaming rubble, burned and exploded Luddite soldiers, and hunks of twisted metal. All Constance's—and the armor's—handiwork. The building in the center of the island was still standing, though its door had been blasted open.

'What are you waiting for?' Darius asked, detaching the vest and running forward. 'Blow it up.'

'Can't,' Constance answered him, startling all of them with the ferocity of her voice through the armor's speakers. 'It would be impossible to find the device under that much rubble.'

Darius swore. Of *course* it wasn't that easy.

'This is my show now, then,' Malik said smoothly. 'Constance, you're our cover. Stay between us and any fields of fire at all times. Use explosives if you have to, but remember you're our defensive line. Darius, Leon, you two stay near me and try to do what you can. Now *move*.'

As they rushed toward the prison's blasted entrance, Darius couldn't help hoping that Bianca was still okay.

Chapter Twenty-Five

00:25 remaining

'And here they are,' Ludd said softly, his eyes narrowed. 'It's sad, but I did give them a choice.'

'What do you mean?' Bianca asked carefully, keeping her eyes on the monitors. She assumed Constance was inside the armor, which meant the three people barely visible behind her were Malik, Leon, and Darius. Lights flashed all over the armor's plating as hundreds of bullets ricocheted off. Every few seconds one of Constance's weapons would activate, forcing the Luddites on the other cameras to duck behind cover. Malik and Darius used these opportunities to lean out from behind Constance and fire a few carefully placed shots. There was a bank of monitors on the left wall, each showing a live feed of the cameras in individual Luddites' helmets. Nearly a quarter went dark in a matter of seconds.

'I left your friends a choice between confronting me and escaping before their window closes. They have chosen death, but then, that has always been the appeal of child soldiers.'

Constance's armor stuttered to a stop, and its red eye went dark. A shower of sparks flew up from its right side. Had a bullet made it through a weakened plate, or had the thing finally just broken down? Bianca bit her lip and prayed that it was at least still functional enough to open and let Constance escape. Leon pulled something out of his bag and threw it into a rapidly approaching group of Luddites. It exploded in a flash of brilliant, blinding light. Bianca winced and looked away from the monitors. Ludd was sitting back calmly, his eyes closed.

'Children think they are invincible, that death is something that happens to other people. They are aggressive and emotionally confused. They will latch onto anything that allows them to act out their anger and fear while providing a sense of meaning.'

The cameras flickered back on, revealing a dozen

white-armored men clustering around the abandoned armor as they searched for the team. Bianca stifled a cheer. A monitor off to the side showed Darius helping Malik climb a ladder to the second tier of cells. Once they were all safely up, Constance pushed something the size of a television remote. Bianca turned back to the first monitor, where the plating around the armor's weapons was glowing angrily. The Luddites surrounding it didn't have enough time to get away before the armor detonated.

'Children think they know more than adults,' Ludd said, a new edge to his voice. He gave her a disgusted sidelong look, and she swallowed dryly. 'You foolish, silly girl. Of course I knew about the transmitter in your ear. I had to test your loyalty, didn't I?' Bianca reached for her gun but he was up in an instant, a pistol pressed into her forehead. 'You failed.'

Bianca glanced over his shoulder. More men had arrived on the catwalks. The team had retreated into one of the cells. She had to act soon.

'You sure do think you know a lot,' she said with a smile. 'In fact, you might be the most arrogant person I've ever met.' Then in a single, smooth motion, she kicked her injured leg straight up into Ludd's chin, sending him tumbling over his chair. He fell in a heap and groaned, not getting up.

Bianca quickly snatched the cables out of some nearby monitors and used them to bind his wrists and ankles, tying him tight to his chair. He came to just as she was finishing and spat at her feet.

'This was your plan? What was the *point*?'

'I was slowing down the team,' she said. 'I was afraid we could never find the device unless I tricked you into bringing me to it. I thought that maybe if I got you to reveal its location, I could get some kind of hint back to them.'

'You don't want freedom, then?'

'More than you could ever know,' Bianca said. 'Just not at your price.'

She looked again at the monitor. The Luddites had reached the cell where the team was barricaded, but they were being held at bay by a few well-ricocheted grenades. Those would run out soon, though. 'I liked the part where I got to kick you too,' she said as she sat in Ludd's chair and pulled up to one of the room's command terminals. 'That was pretty nice.'

'You couldn't have known the EM resonator was in this room—'

'I guessed,' Bianca said. She looked around, and for the first time noticed another dark chrome box resting near a bank of servers. 'I know I'm just a bloodthirsty little child soldier, but I'm not stupid.'

'And you didn't know your friends were coming,' he fumed. 'What were you going to do, *wrestle* my ultimate weapon into submission?'

216

'Honestly?' Bianca said, smiling as she found the command she'd been looking for. 'I was making it up as I went along. I learned from the best.' She looked at the monitors again, making sure Darius was still alive.

She kicked Ludd again for good measure, knocking him out completely this time, and hit the return key.

Chapter Twenty-Six

00:14 remaining

Twilight poured in through the windows, casting the shadows of the cell's iron bars across Darius and the rest of the team, making them look like a combination of skeletons and inmates. The sound of dozens of boots echoed in the hallway, counting down the last few moments of Darius's life. They were out of grenades. Darius was almost out of bullets.

Any second now, he thought. Someone touched his right hand. He looked up to see Constance smiling. Malik did the same, firmly taking his left while hugging Leon.

'We tried,' Constance said. 'I'm proud of us.'

'Me, too,' Darius said. Tears prickled at the corners of his eyes. 'It's been an honor, guys.'

Just as he was about to step out into the cell block and start shooting, a series of clicks echoed down the hall, and the lights went out one by one. There was an ear-piercing screech as the intercom came to life.

'Turn right out of the cell,' Bianca's voice echoed around them. 'Go *now*.'

Darius didn't hesitate. He charged and heard the others follow. He collided with a body encased in hardened synthetic armor, but he spun around it and kept moving. Someone yelled. He thought he heard Constance and Leon run ahead.

'Malik!' he hissed loudly, waving his hands in the darkness. Someone grabbed his hand and limped toward him, whispering thanks. Darius took Malik's weight onto his shoulder and ran as fast as he could in the direction Bianca had given them. Flashes of light popped behind them as the Luddites regained their senses and fired. The shots all went wide, pinging off the iron bars of the cells to either side.

'Keep going straight,' Bianca instructed, 'straight again, left, right, left, straight, and through the door.'

His heart pounding, trying to dodge the bullets coming from behind, Darius did as he was told. He had trouble keeping track of where he was in the instructions, and Malik stumbled a few times, but they kept doggedly moving forward. Finally they saw a rectangle of light ahead, and pushed themselves to sprint the last few feet. Ludd's soldiers weren't far behind.

'Just leave me,' Malik gasped.

'Why do people keep asking me to do that?' Darius snapped, dragging his hurt companion behind him. He shoved Malik through the door and slammed it shut just as a rain of bullets hit it, leaving dents up and down its surface. Constance turned the deadbolt and leaned against a nearby wall, panting. Darius blinked slowly in the bright light.

'Hi,' Bianca said. She pointed to a black cube next to a bank of servers. Darius noticed that what had been a long red progress bar on all the other devices had been reduced to a few pixels. 'We're down to less than a minute.'

Leon and Constance sprinted to the device and tossed their tool bags onto the floor, moving faster than Darius had ever seen them. Ludd's men slammed something into the door, warping the metal. There were a few moments of silence, punctuated by a buzzing noise and Leon swearing under his breath as he apparently tripped a security measure, and then the door blew backward. Luddite soldiers rushed in. Darius shot wildly while Malik took more precise aim behind him. Luddites fell, but more charged over them. Darius's weapon clicked. He heard Malik's do the same.

Bianca lifted her gun, closed one eye, and pulled her trigger twelve times in rapid succession. Silence followed, punctuated this time by a sigh of relief from Constance.

'We did it,' she said.

Chapter Twenty-Seven

00:02 remaining

'Sorry about shooting you,' Bianca said, smiling weakly at Leon.

Leon grunted and resumed packing up his tools. Bianca noticed that he was working with a level of precision and care unusual even for him. She wondered if it was some kind of ritual, a way of coping with the idea that these were the last few minutes of his life. Constance walked over to Malik and rested her hand on his, but he brushed it away. Bianca clenched her teeth, and Constance looked heartbroken for a moment, but after a second of hesitation, Malik took Constance in his arms and held her tight.

Darius just stood next to Bianca, one arm braced against a nearby console, staring off into space.

'Oberon will make sure she gets closure,' she said softly, putting a hand on his arm.

'What?'

'The girl in the apartment. They'll make sure she knows you died doing *something* heroic, even if she doesn't know exactly what.'

'Like she would believe I could ever do something like this.' Darius ran a hand through his hair. 'I guess things change pretty fast. Speaking of which, look at you! That was one of the best cons I've ever seen. You're a fast learner.'

'I was hoping you'd figure it out once you realized I said, "It's been fun."' She smiled ruefully. 'The others will agree, *fun* isn't a word I use often.'

'How did you know they would accept your offer?'

'Well, he obviously knew Oberon had time travel,' she said, gesturing to Ludd's prone form. 'Their armor and weapons were close to ours. And, though I didn't realize it at the time, he knows enough about doors to disable them remotely. I guessed that somebody had been feeding him information, but not enough to keep us from beating him in every city. So I figured he would be desperate for more information, for a better informant.

But it's all thanks to you. Good job on figuring out the mole thing in the first place.'

'Rewind for a second,' Darius said, 'to the part about the doors being deactivated remotely?'

'Yeah,' Bianca said, shrugging. 'So what?'

'Did he do it from this room?'

'Probably. If this isn't a nerve center I'm not sure what is.'

'Leon,' Darius said, 'I want you to figure out what he did, and I want to know five minutes ago.'

Leon nodded and jumped into the nearest workstation, where he started typing like mad.

'Constance,' Darius said. 'What, exactly, goes into making a door?'

'It's like a mini particle accelerator. The trick is sending out a pulse that locks the Chamber onto a set location. All the door does is funnel enough power through a circuit to punch a temporary hole in time and space so that you can move through.'

'What would we need to send a signal?' Darius asked.

'The hijacked radio satellite I just located might work,' Leon said. 'Someone seems to have loaded the frequencies for the entire West Coast on here.'

'But we can't generate enough power to let us through,' Malik said.

Bianca waved at the device. 'Don't those—Ludd called them EM resonators. Don't they suck up tons of power?'

'Yes,' Leon said, turning around. 'But you need two sources to kind of form a circuit with one another.'

'The armor's reactor might work,' Constance said.

'If you hadn't blown it up.'

'Please,' Constance said, rolling her eyes. 'It's a fusion core. Whoever made that was one of the best engineers on the planet. Do you think an engineer would put a self-destruct button in a machine like that if it could cause a massive nuclear fallout?'

'Yes?' they all guessed at once.

'I'm checking,' Constance said. 'If the reactor's intact you owe me fifty dollars!'

Leon rubbed his neck as she hurried out of the room. 'There's still one problem.'

'Of course there is,' Darius said.

'It's not just the power requirements that make the doors so hard to create. There's a lot of higher-order theoretical mathematics involved, a lot of brain-bending quantum theory I don't even pretend to understand. Without a *lot* of careful work, I'm talking months if not years, a punch through to the Chamber can be incredibly unstable.'

'Unstable how?'

'We've been sent back a few times to stop our own engineers from setting up doors that would break down,' Bianca said. 'When they break, they tend to kind of . . . *dissolve* all the matter in a one-mile radius into a fine sand.'

'So what?' Darius asked, jerking his chin toward Ludd's prone form. 'No one is on this island except us and him. And frankly, if he dissolves into sand, it'll be better than he deserves.'

'Agreed,' said Leon. 'But there's still no guarantee we'll make it through before the break.'

'We die either way,' Bianca said, spinning in Ludd's command chair, grinning widely. 'I say we do it.'

'Me, too,' Malik agreed.

'Okay,' Leon said, scratching his chin. 'But this all rests on Constance being right, which is—'

'How's it taste?' Constance yelled from outside the door. She stumbled over the heap of Luddites with a faceted steel ball held triumphantly over her head. 'How's it taste to *lose*, Leon?'

'Never mind.' He sighed. 'I'm not sure I want to live anymore.'

'Get to work anyway,' Bianca said.

Chapter Twenty-Eight

00:00 remaining

'This is it,' Constance said, holding two wires close together. Blue lightning arced hungrily between the twin metal points.

'Pulse sent,' Leon said. 'Connection forming *now*.'

Constance touched the wires together, and the metal immediately fused as the armor's reactor and the EM resonator's power source began to feed off each other. The room filled with a low buzz that made Darius's teeth itch. He tapped Bianca's shoulder and pointed to Ludd, still passed out in the chair.

'Are you sure we can't take him?' he asked, the crackling, howling wind of the reactors stealing most of his voice.

She shook her head, her hair whipping around her face.

'I'd like to,' she said. 'Believe me. I want him interrogated. But we have no idea how long our window will be, and he's not worth the extra millisecond.'

Darius chewed his lip and gave the man another look. He was their only lead on locating the traitor inside Oberon. Who had been feeding secrets to Ludd?

'Don't dwell on it,' Bianca said.

She grabbed his shoulder. Blue light flashed across her face as lightning crackled from the floor to the ceiling, tracing an erratic circular shape in the air between the reactor and the EM resonator. A white-bordered oval wavered into view, like a giant egg made of light and color. It seemed flat, but when Darius leaned from side to side, it somehow retained its dimensions from every angle. The interior of the Chamber was just visible inside the light. There were people standing on the other side, their faces hidden by the border of the opening.

'Injured first!' Darius said.

Malik and Bianca both shot him disgusted looks, but neither was stupid enough to waste time. There was only enough room in the tear for two people to pass through at once, and it was getting smaller by the moment. Leon and Constance went through next.

The light began to fade, and the portal's borders quivered, threatening to close. Darius ran forward and dove through it, stumbling to the Chamber's smooth floor just as a thundering roar split through the air. He glanced back and watched as the island on the other side of the portal dissolved like a sugar cube in warm water.

And then the portal was gone, as though it had never existed, leaving silence and a faint smell of battery acid in its wake. Darius tried to stand but ended up falling unsteadily back to his knees. He settled for watching the single door in the tiny, circular room.

A second later the door tore open, and Agent Grosz hurried in, followed by four nurses. She looked almost as bad as they did. 'Good work, team,' she said, smiling warmly. 'I'm really proud of you.' Darius thought the last part was directed at him, though he couldn't be sure.

'What happens now?' Darius asked.

'You rest,' Grosz told him. 'Who knows when we'll need you to save the world again.'

Bianca reached over and tugged playfully at his hair as the nurses lifted her onto a gurney.

'Good work out there, newbie,' she said, laughing louder than anyone with a shattered knee and a broken foot had a right to. 'Welcome to the team.'

Meredith Stroud

Meredith Stroud lives in Chattanooga, Tennessee with her partner/accomplice. She graduated with an English degree from the University of Tennessee in 2010, where she was published in the *Sequoya Review*. She spends most of her free time whipping up biscuits for hipsters, helping her friends pretend to be elves, and raising a little girl who insists she is actually a car.